T0194626

THE LAST SIN OF
PANCHO MARTINEZ

ROGER SAENZ

authorHOUSE®

AuthorHouse™
1663 Liberty Drive
Bloomington, IN 47403
www.authorhouse.com
Phone: 1 (800) 839-8640

Published by AuthorHouse 08/14/2019

Scripture taken from The Holy Bible, King James Version. Public Domain

ISBN: 978-1-7283-2350-3 (sc)
ISBN: 978-1-7283-2349-7 (e)

Library of Congress Control Number: 2019912210

Print information available on the last page.

To my parents, Heriberto and Josie Saenz, whose
love, commitment, and loyalty to our family
and to the Lord Jesus Christ have inspired me
immeasurably. I deeply love and appreciate you!

CONTENTS

CHAPTER 1

ANOTHER MAN'S BED, ANOTHER MAN'S WIFE

As the sun began to set, the dark clouds appeared from the edge of town where Pancho Martinez, a ruggedly handsome Mexican American male, was lying down in another man's bed with that man's wife. The cold December night was so dry that a person could taste the stale air in the sweaty bedroom.

"Pancho Martinez you'd better go now! I wouldn't want my husband to catch us like this!" exclaimed Stella as she pointed to their stark-naked bodies.

Stella was the kind of woman who had had it tough all of her life. Every Chicano knows someone who is a Stella or has an aunt or other relative who is a Stella. She's the kind of woman that is always looking for love, but it is evident that love isn't looking for her. You've seen the Stellas of the world. You run into them at the Walmart on Friday nights around midnight when you go to pick up a last-minute item that can't wait for the following day. As she walks by with that West Coast strut, you can't help but look at the way she

1

proudly sways her hips. It's almost hypnotic and intoxicating at the same time. She has a noble arrogance about her as well as a beautiful face, but if you look deep into her eyes, you can see the weight of despair and empty thoughts of a jagged life. She has a great figure with all the right curves, which makes you wonder if she goes to the gym or runs laps around the park at Woodlawn Lake. Anyone who knows her, though, knows that she doesn't work out at all. It's her Aztec ancestry and her mother's Mexican manners that give her that shapely body and charm that she can't help but show.

Stella was young and most often lonely—a little girl who was almost a lady. She grew up too fast to keep up with herself; consequently, she ended up married when she turned thirteen. Her husband told her that he loved her, and he promised to take care of her for the rest of her life. He promised her the world in order to be able to wake up every morning and gaze at her beautiful face next to his. But then the drinking started. Her husband would get drunk and falsely accuse her of sexual unfaithfulness and treachery. He would hit and mistreat her like an old lopsided punching bag that is hanging in the garage and only gets used when frustrations need to be purged because your wife doesn't let you stay out late with the boys. Stella left that marriage after one year and one baby and remarried at age sixteen. She thought that it would be different this time. It wasn't.

At the age of twenty, she married for the third time. She wasn't even sure why she did it. It wasn't for love, and it wasn't for money. Her friends and family had pressured her into it, or at least that's what she thought. During family gatherings on Thanksgiving, Easter, or a niece's birthday party, her aunts would tell her that she'd better get married or she would end up old and alone like them. "Find yourself a nice young man while you still can," her *tia* Chela would always tell her.

This marriage lasted longer than the others, but in the end, she walked away just like she knew she would.

After some years and many affairs and romances, she found herself in her thirties as a tired woman and a mother of three children, each with a different father and different last names. Then she married for the fourth time. Life had given her a deep, bitter cup, and she didn't want to drink from it anymore. She was about to give up on love, and then her heart got a new start when she met Pancho Martinez.

Pancho Martinez was George Clooney, Elvis Presley, Luis Miguel, and Brad Pitt all rolled up in one man. He was the epitome of a modern-day Casanova, Romeo, and the jack of hearts. He was the man all women wanted to love and loved to want. Have you ever seen a movie where the bad guy in the story is the main character and the writers want you to be on his side and admire him? They want you to see life from his point of view. They want you to get to know him, see him as a hero and fall in love with him. You learn to love him because you learn to understand him. Sure, he may have committed a murder or two, or robbed a bank, but he had good reasons for committing those crimes. Down deep inside, he's really a hero. He's like Moses, who murdered an Egyptian and then was promoted by God to lead the great and miraculous Exodus that freed an entire nation from four hundred years of unforgiving, unfathomable, and unpleasant slavery. Pancho Martinez however, was no saint. He'd learned about life on the hard, dirty streets of the city. His life motto was, "I do what I like, and I like what I do."

"What are you talking about, sweet Marie? Didn't you say that your husband was going to be working late tonight? What do you mean you don't want him to catch us like this?" Pancho Martinez sneered.

Stella ground her teeth in disgust and pushed Pancho Martinez with both hands as hard as she could while her face took on the look of an angered silverback gorilla. With her nostrils flaring, her eyes glistening with hostility, the skin on her forehead wrinkled, and with all the emotion she could summon, she said, "What do you mean, 'sweet Marie?' You know that my name is Stella!"

She was seriously upset with Pancho Martinez, but he wasn't fazed by her disorganized attempt to hit him. How much damage could a girl do to a healthy, rugged man while she was lying naked on a bed bought in a South Side garage sale?

Stella was angry because Pancho Martinez called her Marie. But he knew her name. He was only doing what he did all the time. You see, Pancho Martinez was a romantic at heart. He was always quoting lines from songs, movies, or books that he'd read. Sometimes he quoted some lines in inopportune circumstances, and people misunderstand his intentions. They didn't see the humor or the romance that was intended. But sometimes he quoted lines that made him appear to be thoughtful, wise, sublime, and intriguing. This was one of those instances. He was quoting a Bob Dylan line. But Stella obviously had not heard much of Bob Dylan. Pancho Martinez was aware of her pop culture ignorance and attempted to move on with the conversation.

"Look, Stella, my feet have barely gotten warm and now you are telling me to leave. Why don't you just relax and do what you do best? If there were an event in the Olympics for this, I'm sure you would win a gold medal."

Stella was again agitated with Pancho Martinez's manners. "You dirty rat! Is that all that you want me for?"

Pancho Martinez wanted to continue to lovingly tease Stella, so he used another line. "I'm not a mouse. I'm a man! You know that I . . . . . I . . . . . I care for you."

Pancho Martinez was not afraid to use the word *love*, like the Fonz from the *Happy Days* show who couldn't say, "I love you" to any of his girlfriends. The fact was that he didn't love Stella. He wanted to be honest, but he also didn't want to hurt her feelings. He really liked Stella. She was his favorite–at least for the time being. "Stella, why don't you just shut up and give me a kiss," Pancho uttered amorously.

Stella reacted to these words like any welfare mother would. Her demeanor and her thoughts quickly changed. She gazed into Pancho Martinez's deep, brown eyes, smiled lovingly, and gave him a passionate "you make me feel like I'm sixteen again" kiss.

The moment froze in time for the two lovebirds as they kissed and warmly embraced.

❧ CHAPTER 2 ❧

THE ANGRY, JEALOUS HUSBAND

Suddenly, the door burst open and an angry, disheveled, pudgy, balding, one-pay-check-away-from-poor-white-trash, Anglo American husband rushed into the bedroom brandishing an enormous pistol like Clint Eastwood in a Dirty Harry movie. His pants and shirt were too small. His zipper and buttons were screaming for mercy as they held on with all the strength they could muster.

Stella's husband had suspected something sinful and wicked. He had noticed how Stella had been cold and distant toward him in the recent months. She had been as distant as the sun and as cold as liquid oxygen. He came home early this evening hoping to find Stella alone, but he wasn't sure if he would so he'd brought his .44 magnum pistol with him just in case. If Stella was sleeping with another man, he was going to deal with him with as much fury as possible. He really loved Stella. He knew that she had slept with other men in the past, but this didn't matter to him. He knew that she had children from other men, but this also didn't matter to him. Stella was the woman that he had been waiting for all his life. Upon meeting her, he quickly asked her to marry him, and when she said yes, he had been ecstatic. He was Stella's fourth husband, but Stella was his first wife and his queen. He was not about to let anything or anyone ruin his relationship with the queen of all his dreams.

The angry, jealous husband entered the dreary room with the immense, cold blue steel gun in his right hand. He immediately raised it up and pointed it at Pancho Martinez. His eyes were on fire! You could feel the jealousy and hatred streaming out from his eyes across the room toward Pancho. His entire body felt numb and cold at the same time. He stiffened up like an old board on a picket fence. He didn't have the guts or the courage to kill a man. But he had to go through with this. He had to stand up for what rightfully belonged to him. He had to stand up for his Stella!

He felt a knot begin to swell up in his throat. He felt a trickle of sweat run down his forehead. His hands were wet and clammy. He could hardly breathe. He wanted to run. He wanted this to be a bad dream. He wanted all of this to go away. But it was real. This was really happening. His courage had left him, but jealousy spurred him on like an intimidating crowd of teenagers in middle school who would yell, "Are you going to let him do that to you? Show him who you are! Let him know how much he has hurt you!"

With all the rage, anger, wrath, and spit that he could rally he cried out at the top of his lungs, "What is going on here? Who are you? That is my wife that you are manhandling!"

Pancho Martinez had seen a gun pointed at his face

before. This was not the first time and it probably would not be the last. He was not afraid to die, and he was not afraid of the angry, jealous husband. Pancho Martinez stood up exposing his strong, naked body and answered the man, "My name is Pancho Martinez. Today is a good day to die" (another line he had heard on TV).

The jealous husband shouted with disgust, "You fool; I'll kill you for this!" Then he awkwardly pulled back the hammer of the gun with his sweaty, grimy, chubby thumb. Pancho's heart and mind had begun to race. He reached down to the floor and picked up his greasy, gasoline smelling 501 Levi's blue jeans and calmly put them on. He contemplated the situation and it didn't look good for the hero. He had heard people say that when you are faced with death your entire life flashes before your eyes. At that moment, as he stared down the barrel of the .44 magnum, Pancho felt the walls closing in on him. He felt alone and abandoned. The only thing he thought of at that moment in time, was to speak with God.

In an instant, and oblivious to the gun yielding madman, he reached deep into his soul and spirit and started a conversation with Jesus. Not the blue-eyed, pretty-boy Jesus that has hung over the fire place at your tia's house. Pancho began to speak with the true and living God that the bible talks about.

Pancho had heard of other gods and of other religions, but he did not want to speak with Buddha, Vishnu, or Allah. He wanted to speak with the God of the bible. Pancho whispered, "Well God, I guess this is it. I guess it's time for me to die. I never thought it would end like this. I know that I caused a lot of heartache and pain in my time, but life is hard and unfair. That's just the way things are. I don't regret anything that I ever did. Everybody deserved what they got. I wasn't that bad. My life wasn't that bad."

As Pancho stared down the long, sturdy barrel of the .44 magnum, he heard a distant cry of a newborn infant.

⇥ CHAPTER 3 ⇤

TELL ME WHO YOUR FRIENDS ARE, AND I'LL TELL YOU WHO YOU ARE

"*Haaayyyyyy mamacita,*" screeched a tired, aching, naked woman sprawled out on an operating room table while she clenched a dirty rag between her teeth. With one final push she delivered a bloody, screaming child. Olivia Martinez, wife of Alberto Martinez, gave birth to her fourth son at the *Robert B. Green* hospital in down town San Antonio, Texas.

The total delivery fee for the baby was twenty-five dollars and two pints of blood. The name "Pancho" had been chosen for the newly arrived bundle of joy because his parents wanted to stay away from the typical, hard to pronounce, hard on the ear, Mexican names of their ancestors. They wanted something uncomplicated, yet Hispanic. Thus Pancho, no middle name, Martinez had been introduced into God's human race on an otherwise uneventful day.

Pancho and his family had resided in the Alazan-Apache

Homes Government Housing Projects in the West Side of San Antonio. The West Side predominantly consisted of a Spanish-speaking, Hispanic population. In general, Hispanic fathers were viewed as the providers, protectors, and macho do-as-I-say-not-as-I-do heavy-handed disciplinarians of the family. Mothers were the loving, caring, you-better-eat-all-of-your-peas, sensible, listeners of the family. At the age of six, Pancho's family moved to the South Side of San Antonio.

The South Side was vastly different from the West Side. English was the prominent language in the South Side. Everyone lived in houses, and not in governmental housing complexes. The neighborhood children had dreams of driving hot rods or Harley-Davidson's instead of the West Side stereotypical lowriders. Rock and roll filled the airwaves instead of the tear jerking, I-want-to-drown-in-a-bottle-because-my-spouse-just-left-me Spanish music of the West Side.

Pancho Martinez excelled in his educational training in elementary school and was quite the lady's man. His Spanish speaking abilities were all but lost in the anglicized neighborhood. He had some Anglo American neighbors that would invite him and his brothers to Sunday school at a nearby Baptist Church. This was the first time Pancho had heard about Jesus and his sacrificial love for humanity. He enjoyed hearing and learning about the gentle healer from Galilee named Jesus.

His Anglo neighbors included teenagers such as beautiful ZZ, her gorgeous sister Liz, Travis the all-American sportsman, and young children his own age such as crazy cousin Nicky, Jonathan, and his sister June Ann.

There was a good reason why Nicky was called "Crazy." He really was crazy.

When Pancho Martinez, at the age of six, first met Crazy Nicky they got into a fist fight. Pancho walked outside of his house on a hot summer morning to see if there were any neighborhood children willing to play. Pancho was accustomed to being surrounded by children when they lived in the West side projects.

He laid eyes on Crazy Nicky and walked right up to this little pudgy, sandy-haired stranger and the first words out of Crazy Nicky's mouth were, "I bet I can beat the tar out of you."

Pancho was stunned by this phrase, but of course he was no stranger to fighting. He had several rounds of fighting underneath his belt from the West side.

The two little boys commenced to hurl fists at each other and kick and scream. Crazy Nicky knocked Pancho to the ground and began to shove handfuls of dirt and pebbles into Pancho's mouth. This enraged Pancho so he cleverly flipped Crazy Nicky onto the ground. Pancho then proceeded to shove dirt into Nicky's mouth. Suddenly they both stood up gagging and spitting out dirt and pebbles. They took a hard look into each other's eyes and said what all six-year-old boys say after a rugged fist fight, "Let's go play."

This was the beginning of a beautiful friendship. Life seemed trouble-free and simple for young Pancho until he arrived in sixth grade Middle School.

At Thomas Nelson Page Middle School, Pancho had met many new friends who lived in the Victoria Courts government housing just south of down town San Antonio. These new friends brought drugs to school, regularly practiced truancy, were involved sexually, and appeared to have had a good time doing all of these illicit activities. Pancho immediately got involved with them and all of their ghastly deeds.

Pancho was intelligent and an above average learner. His studies came natural to him. He excelled in his schoolwork and as a result, he was seen as a leader by his peers. He was cool, smart, athletic, good-looking, and all of thirteen.

His inner circle of close friends and pot-smoking buddies included blonde-haired Mario (only his mother knows where this Chicano acquired blonde hair), Charles (always liked to fight), Fat Fēfē (an excellent basketball player in spite of being overweight), Jabber Jaws Anthony (liked to guzzle hard liquor for fun), Disco Henry (a ladies man with above average good looks who liked to dance), Psycho Michael (impulsive and a menace to society), Stoner (always wanted to smoke pot), Andrew (Pancho's close friend since the age of six), Mōn (a great athlete), and of course, Crazy Nicky.

Pancho's first official girlfriend was a beautiful young girl who had exquisite eyes and jet-black hair named Barbara Jean. Pancho had met her at a *quinceañera*. Barbara Jean was seated across the dance hall from Pancho. Pancho noticed that she had been looking at him. Pancho had also been looking at her.

Barbara Jean was stunning! Her romantic passion had shown like the brightest fire upon her innocent face. She had her head held high. Her striking eyes were piercing across the room with determination. When her eyes had met with Pancho's eyes she smiled. Pancho had become captivated.

Barbara Jean was young and sweet. But she also had a sinister and seductive side to her. She had developed earlier than most girls her age and she would use this to her advantage. With an alluring smile and some cleavage, she would drive all the young boys crazy. She would do this just for kicks. She would do this because she could.

Barbara Jean was the first among many girlfriends and loves for Pancho Martinez. The sex, drugs, and rock and roll had become a way of life during his early years.

❧ CHAPTER 4 ❧

THE PARTY LIFE

It had been the days of wine and roses for Pancho and his friends. Life was one big middle school party. The alcohol and drugs had begun to be a part of his everyday life. They had begun to consume his every thought.

One hot summer night in May, Pancho and his friends had heard about a middle school graduation party in a neighborhood near Pecan Valley Park. Pecan Valley was not Pancho's neighborhood. But he and his friends knew that the girls there would be friendly twentieth century foxes.

The party would have been like most on the South Side of San Antonio. There would be plenty of alcohol, weed, and three girls for every boy. Most parties would have been held in someone's back yard and with parental permission. Some girls would show up on the hot summer nights looking spicy with their terry cloth tube tops and short shorts. Others would show up with tight blue jeans and a Black Sabbath tee shirt.

The music was always loud at these South Side parties. The airwaves were filled with Judas Priest, AC/DC, Budgie,

Scorpions, Black Sabbath, Van Halen, Moxy, April Wine, Rush, Blue Oyster Cult, Garfield, Legs Diamond, Thin Lizzy, UFO, Riot, and many other 1970's hard rock favorites. The teenage attendees would be head banging and sharing legendary tales of their adventures in the wonderland they called middle school.

On occasion there would have been some soft, slow music such as Lionel Richie's "Easy," so the partiers could pair up with the opposite sex and slow dance.

Thirteen-year-old Pancho and his friends had shown up uninvited and crashed the party. "I told you dudes that this was going to be a cool party," exclaimed Pancho as he and his band of friends entered the back yard and setting of the party.

Stoner quickly had taken notice of all the young scantily clad girls, "Hey man, look at all the chicks!"

Psycho had had his eyes on something else, "Hey man, look at all the beer!"

Fat Fēfē's attention was on something else too, "Man, look at all that delicious food!"

Pancho had raised his arms like a policeman directing traffic and said, "Hey, why don't you all just calm down and relax. Come on; let's go get some beer."

Pancho had always been a smooth operator in any and every situation. He was a regular Rico suave. He was fine as wine and good as wood. As the gang of young thugs had begun to walk into the party many of the girls started flirting with Pancho. And of course, Pancho gave his best smooth talk to each of the girls as he passed by them, "Hi gorgeous. Hey Baby. You're looking good. I'll catch you in a minute. Save the last dance for me, *masota* (beautiful)."

The boys walked up to the ice-cold keg of Budweiser beer and they each grabbed an eighteen-ounce clear, plastic cup and filled them up with the intoxicating beverage. They all stood around the keg and waited for their next move. They stood silently gulping the beer and attempted to look cool and refined.

Suddenly, Fat Fēfē busted out, "Hey man, I'm hungry, let's go get something to eat! Just look at all that food just sitting there waiting for us to eat it."

Pancho gave the order, "Okay, let's all make our way over to the table and get something to eat."

They all walked slowly over to the table stocked with huge pots of chicken *mole*, rice, beans, and piles of bread loaves to dip in the mole sauce. There was also a table filled with ham sandwiches, bologna sandwiches, and cheese sandwiches.

The stereo record player was blaring. A string of multi-colored Christmas lights strung from tree branches illuminated the back yard. A strobe light was piercing the darkness near some purple and crimson crepe myrtle bushes in full bloom. Pancho and his troop had taken aim at the sandwich table because it would be easier to look cool eating a sandwich while standing up than eating chicken mole and getting the mole sauce all over your face and clothes.

They were all astonished as they stared at the sandwiches professionally cut and prepared by the Alamo Heights H-E-B Central Market on Broadway street near Brackenridge Park. They then started to dig into the sandwiches. Fat Fēfē grabbed two sandwiches, one in each hand, and began attacking them, "These sure are good sandwiches. There is enough here to feed an army. Can we take some home with us?"

Psycho chimed in next, "Yeah man, I need to take some home to my six brothers and sisters. The welfare check was late again this month, so we don't have anything to eat at home."

Psycho started to put sandwiches into his pockets while Fat Fēfē stuffed his jacket full of sandwiches. Fat Fēfē always wore a jacket. He wore a thin, light weight, black golf jacket. It didn't matter if it was the middle of summer; he still wore his jacket. And it wasn't because he was cold. During the summer, it would regularly get up to one hundred degrees in San Antonio. Fēfē wore the jacket as a fashion statement. It was his way of looking cool. After the boys had loaded up on sandwiches, Pancho's next order was to go talk to some girls.

They saw a group of girls standing nearby so they all walked over to introduce themselves. "Hi girls, my name is Pancho Martinez and these are my friends. I hope you are ready to have a good time."

One of the girls, Jungle Jackie, was quite attractive. She was tall and slender, with long curly black hair. She had been wearing faded blue jeans and a string halter top that was bright yellow and extremely revealing. Jungle Jackie asked, "What kind of a good time?"

She was called Jungle Jackie because she could mimic the call of the Australian kookaburra bird precisely. This was the loud shrieking jungle bird sound that was heard in the old Tarzan movies. Stoner quickly replied, "The best kind of good time" as he pulled out an ounce of Panama Red marijuana.

All the girls were thrilled about the Panama Red

marijuana because they had heard stories about the bright, rusty red marijuana but had never actually seen it. Each girl went up to one of the guys and put their arm around them. Jungle Jackie went straight for Pancho and began to kiss him on the lips with great fervor.

After a moment Jungle Jackie had come up for air and whispered into Pancho's ear, "You are a very good kisser. How come I haven't met you before?"

Pancho replied, "Hey baby, all the girls tell me the same thing. That's just the way God made me."

As the boys had continued to interact with the girls, the jealous boyfriend of Jungle Jackie, Toné Loco, walked slowly toward Pancho. Toné Loco, along with five of his friends, stood directly in front of Pancho and Jungle Jackie and exclaimed with fire in his eyes, "Who do you think you are? And what do you think you are doing kissing my girlfriend?"

Jungle Jackie quickly and rudely answered him, "Hey Toné Loco, why don't you just leave me alone? You don't own me and I'm not your girlfriend! I can kiss whoever I want to kiss!"

Toné Loco had been completely embarrassed. He became enraged even more by Jungle Jackie's response and lack of respect for him. "You better just shut up Jackie," Toné Loco barked.

He then proceeded to swing his right arm and slapped Jungle Jackie squarely on the face. Everyone had been caught off guard by his action except for Pancho. The girls screamed in horror and ran off into the darkened night.

Pancho gently pulled Jungle Jackie away from her enraged boyfriend's reach. Then he stepped up into Toné

Loco's face and boldly said, "My name is Pancho Martinez. I wasn't kissing your girlfriend; she was kissing me."

Toné Loco, who had already been full of anger and hatred toward Pancho shouted, "No one talks to me like that!"

He then pulled out a huge buck knife and lunged at Pancho attempting to stab him in the chest. Pancho instinctively moved out of the way of the incoming knife. Toné Loco's knife had missed Pancho's chest by inches. Pancho instantly reacted and punched Toné Loco in the face with a straight right cross; followed by a short, left hook; and another right to the face.

Toné Loco was stunned at Pancho's hand speed. The three hard blows Pancho had thrown wobbled Toné Loco and caused him to go down to the ground on his hands and knees. Pancho's friends and the other jealous boyfriends had begun to engage in the fight as well.

Two guys literally jumped on Pancho. Stoner picked up a chair and had begun to swing it at everybody and anybody. Psycho and Crazy Nicky were taking turns punching one of the jealous boyfriends on the face. Fat Fēfē ran over to help Pancho but was stopped in his tracks by Toné Loco who was still holding the old timer buck knife in his hand. Toné Loco had the look of a mad man on Green Goddess LSD upon his face.

Toné Loco had cleared his throat, proceeded to spit on the ground, then he shouted at Fat Fēfē, "This is the end of the line for you Fat boy!"

Toné Loco swung the knife in a slashing manner in order to cut his plump opponent. Fat Fēfē stepped back in order to avoid the knife. It barely missed him. Toné Loco kept slashing at him with the knife until Fat Fēfē had been backed up onto the food tables and fell on top of them.

The rest of Pancho's gang was fighting the jealous boyfriends, so they had not seen Fat Fēfē's predicament and thus were unable to help him. Toné Loco approached Fat Fēfē's motionless body sprawled on top of the table and said, "I told y'all not to mess with me! This is what happens when you mess with Toné Loco!"

Toné Loco then proceeded to stab Fat Fēfē repeatedly in the chest area. Fat Fēfē had begun to yell at the top of his lungs in extreme pain. Everyone else stopped what they were doing and stared at the stabbing of Fat Fēfē.

Pancho ran over and kicked Toné Loco in the groin and punched him on the face, one-two. Pancho then took the knife away from Toné Loco's hand and proceeded to beat him viciously and repeatedly with his fists. Toné Loco fell unconscious and bleeding on the dirt.

Pancho was exhausted. He caught his breath long enough to say, "Does anyone else want to go next?" The jealous boyfriends looked at Pancho and were trembling in their black, Red Wing biker boots; then they turned and ran away.

Pancho had looked over at his friend lying motionless on the ground and said, "Fat Fēfē! Get up man!"

Psycho went over to Pancho and sorrowfully said, "He's dead man! He's dead!"

Stoner yelled out, "Let's get out of here! We've got to jet out of here before the police show up!"

Pancho had ignored their pleas and focused on his wounded friend, "Get up Fēfē! You've got to get up!"

Pancho kneeled down. Then he picked up Fat Fēfē's

head to console him. Fat Fēfē looked up with tears in his eyes and extreme pain in his voice and said, "They got me Pancho. They got me good. Tell my mother that I love her. Tell her that she made the best *Carne Guisada* in the world. I'll never taste her homemade tortillas again. I'll never taste her rice *atolé* with raisins on a cold Monday morning again. I'll never . . . . ."

Pancho had cut him off in mid sentence, "Fat Fēfē, is that all that you can talk about at a time like this? You are dying and all you can talk about is food? Let me see what damage they did to you."

Pancho opened up Fat Fēfē's slashed up jacket and all the sandwiches fell out. Everyone was amazed that Fat Fēfē did not have one scratch on him. Toné Loco had only cut up all the sandwiches that Fat Fēfē had previously stuffed into his jacket.

Fat Fēfē exclaimed with joy and surprise, "Hey man, look at that, I'm not bleeding, and I'm not dying. Toné Loco cut up all the sandwiches and didn't even get a scratch on me. You see man; it does pay to be fat and hungry all the time."

Pancho dropped Fat Fēfē's head on the ground and said, "You're crazy man! We thought you were dying."

Stoner looked at all his buddies and said, "We need to steal sandwiches at every party that we go to from now on."

Psycho walked up to Fat Fēfē and asked, "Are those sandwiches still good to eat? Can I take them home?"

Suddenly police sirens were heard in the not so distant background. Pancho gathered his friends and said, "Let's split this joint. We have got to get out of here before the police get here."

They had all started to walk away quickly, but Fat Fēfē returned and picked up two sandwiches and took a big bite out of one of them, then ran off to join his friends.

It seemed like trouble kept sneaking up on Pancho whether he wanted it to or not. The more that trouble knocked on his door, the more hardened, cynical, and calloused he became.

❧ CHAPTER 5 ❧

A DAY IN THE LIFE

The year was 1979. Pancho was fifteen years old and a freshman in High School. Jimmy Carter was president of the United States. Margaret Thatcher had become the British Prime Minister (the first woman to hold the highest office in a European country). The Sony Walkman had been introduced into society. Mother Theresa had won the Nobel Peace Prize.

On one particular day, which had started like any other normal day, tragedy and calamity roared into Pancho's life like an angry tornado fixed on death and destruction.

It was a sunny, but cold morning in November (typical winter weather for San Antonio). The sun had illumined the dingy streets of the South Side of town. The cold, north, Canadian wind had been running chills up and down the spines of Chicanos who were not used to any weather conditions below seventy degrees Fahrenheit.

Pancho had woken up, gotten out of bed, and ran a brush through his mid-back length, straight, black hair. It was the Seventies, and everyone was wearing long hair. Then he made his way to school.

It had been a typical day of dealing with snobbish teachers, lackluster students, and the thing that Pancho liked the most – girl watching. That was one thing that the South Side had had in abundance – beautiful girls. Some girls looked so beautiful and sexy when they strolled by and sashayed their hips that they made everyone looking at them say vowels – *"Ī–ya-yī,"* and "O–my goodness," and "U–sweet thing you!"

At the end of the school day, Pancho had looked for some of his close buddies to see what adventure they could find after school. Pancho ran into his two buddies, Andrew and blonde-haired Mario.

The trio had decided to go to a local neighborhood park called Roosevelt Park. There wasn't anything special about Roosevelt Park. In fact, it was quite small when compared to some of San Antonio's bigger parks such as Brackenridge Park or McAllister Park.

No marathons had ever been held at Roosevelt Park. There were no 5K runs or bike-a-thons either. There were no Martin Luther King, Jr. marches or city-wide protests. There were no *Fiesta* parades or carnival rides. There was, however, a very large swimming pool. It was the focal point of the park. The pool had the capacity to hold hundreds of playful children, overweight moms and dads, bikini clad teenage girls, and ogling teenage boys.

Pancho and some of his friends had, on occasion, snuck into the swimming pool after hours. They had gone late at night for an illegal swim with some local neighborhood girls. Sometimes, the rarely-present Park Rangers would come around and try to arrest the law breakers. Pancho and the other criminals would always outrun the overweight, overworked, and underpaid officers and jump over the pool fence and escape out into the nearby banks of the San Antonio River.

The swimming pool was what had attracted people to the park from miles around. People from the Victoria Courts government housing, people from Nogalitos street, people from Burbank High School, people from Brackenridge High School, and people from the Down Town area would all frequent the friendly cement pond.

It also had some nice make-out spots for those moments when someone needed to have some time alone with that special someone after a date and before you took them home. These were places where someone could learn how to French kiss, make a neck hickie, or hold hands for the first time.

When Pancho, Andrew, and Mario had arrived at the park they were pleasantly surprised to see Pancho's older brother, Pistol Pete and several of his friends (males and females) drinking alcohol and smoking marijuana. Pistol Pete was eight years older than Pancho. Pistol Pete was also the coolest dude anyone could ever have met.

At first, the teenage trio had thought that Pistol Pete and his friends would not let the young whippersnappers hang out with them. When they approached the group, Pistol Pete yelled out and exclaimed to his buddies that his younger brother and his friends were cool and that they could stay and hang out with them. The entire crowd had let out a loud rebel yell and had welcomed the bold trio into their circle of partying.

Pancho and his two close friends had begun to experience

a dream come true by having been allowed to hang out and party with the Big Boy's gang of his notorious and infamous brother, Pistol Pete. Each of the boys had been handed a cold Budweiser can of beer. The marijuana cigarettes had begun to be lit and then passed around. Someone in the group had offered Pancho and his two buddies some LSD, and they gladly partook of it.

After some time, all the beer had been consumed by the large group of revelers. Immediately Pancho, Andrew, and Mario had spoken up and told the group that they would go and retrieve some more beer. Everyone had begun to laugh and jokingly told the young teens that they were not even old enough to legally buy the beer. Pancho and his two buddies, however, had assured the group that they could and would get some more beer.

The three boys had quickly departed from the park and headed toward the nearest convenience store. They arrived at the store and had noticed that there was only one lonely, elderly attendant minding the store. The trio, smoothly and silently, began to walk toward the door where the beer was stored in the cooler.

Each boy had grabbed a case of Budweiser in each hand. Then they had proceeded toward the counter. Their hearts were racing. The adrenaline was in high gear. The drugs and alcohol were spurring them on with fearlessness. They walked pass the counter and held their breath.

Then the three boys made a mad dash toward the exit doors of the store. Mario was the fastest, so he reached the doors first. He pushed as hard as he could with his right shoulder. One of the doors had burst wide open. Andrew and Pancho slid through the open door behind Mario.

The boys were young and athletic and could run like the wind. They had vanished before the store clerk realized what had happened. The daring trio had pulled off the heist. The had gotten away with the theft of six cases of cold Budweiser beer.

Pancho, Mario, and Andrew had arrived back at the park each with a smile from ear to ear. They had meant what they said and said what they meant. They had promised Pistol Pete and his friends that they would get some beer, and they did. Pistol Pete and his friends were ecstatic and could not believe that the young boys had come back with so much beer. Everyone cheered and gave high fives all around. Some of the females danced and jumped with delight. The audacious trio had become the toast of the day and the life of the party.

Pancho contemplated the moment and had said to himself, "Life is good. It doesn't get any better than this."

As soon as the sun had set and darkness had fallen on Roosevelt Park, the trio knew that it was time for them to leave and get back home. They were going to have to sneak into their bedrooms so their parents would not discover their inebriated state of mind.

They had said their farewells and walked away on cloud nine with a can of beer in every pocket. As they walked toward their homes, they realized that they had to finish the beers before their arrival. So, they stopped and entered into an apartment building next to the home of one of Pancho's girlfriends.

The apartment building was a two-story building with a long stairway leading up to the second floor. Pancho and his two companions had stepped into the stairway to get out from the cold and finish the last of the beers. They stood around for a few minutes recounting the events of the day. Pancho had suddenly noticed a young Mexican illegal alien boy, about the same age as he and his friends, walking by on the sidewalk in front of the apartment building.

Pancho had previously seen the boy when he had gone to visit his girlfriend Joann. Joann lived directly adjacent to the apartment building. Pancho had told his friends that he knew the boy. Then Pancho proceeded outside to say hello to him. He didn't know why he wanted to say hello, but he did.

It may have been the drugs, the alcohol, or the euphoric feeling of joy after having pulled off the heist and impressing his brother Pistol Pete that made him go outside. Whatever it was, he went out to say hello to the teenage Mexican boy. Pancho waved his hand in the air at the boy and said in his friendliest voice, "What's up dude?"

The young Mexican boy had turned and looked at Pancho and slowly began to walk toward him. The boy stood directly in front of Pancho and began to speak in Spanish and profane Pancho, his mother, and all of his living relatives. Pancho was stunned at the boy's adverse reaction to his friendly gestures. But then he did what any red-blooded, Mexican American, teenage boy from the South Side of San Antonio would have done in a similar situation – he punched the Mexican illegal boy smack in the face with all the strength that he could muster.

As soon as Pancho had readied himself to deliver a second blow, Blonde-haired Mario flew through the air passed Pancho and pounced on the boy and began to swing his fists feverishly and repeatedly to his face, head, and neck. Pancho had frozen in astonishment at Mario's intervention.

Andrew yelled, "Watch out!" and began to clobber the boy with his belt buckle.

This was no ordinary belt buckle. It was a half inch thick, five inches in diameter, solid stainless-steel plate which weighed about three pounds. The steel plate had been cut into the shape of a German cross. It had a steel loop at one end where a strong leather belt could be attached and held in place by two small metal bolts and nuts. All of Pancho's close friends had a big belt buckle like this. It was their weapon of choice.

The buckle was inconspicuous because it looked like part of a teenage wardrobe. It was also very effective: it could knock someone unconscious with one blow. It could also have kept someone at bay if they were wielding a knife in a combat situation. This had been implemented by Pancho on a previous occasion by swinging the belt and buckle repeatedly like the large blade on a helicopter.

The belt buckles had been introduced to Pancho and his friends by the father of Richard and Robert Ramirez. Their father had been a fabricator at a local sheet metal plant. Pancho and his friends had obtained the buckles for five dollars each. Most of the buckles had been chrome plated for added aesthetic effect.

Andrew swung the belt and buckle and hit the boy on the chest. The boy was wearing a plain white t-shirt and as soon as the buckle hit him, a thin vertical red line appeared upon his shirt. The thin red line had been caused by blood coming out of a gash in his chest caused by the force of the buckle.

Andrew had swung again and hit the boy on the chest which caused an eerie yell of excruciating pain to come out of the boy's mouth. Another thin vertical red line had appeared on the boy's t-shirt. The blood had begun to spread out to the rest of the shirt. The boy had continued to yell hysterically and had fallen to the ground and quickly rolled himself under a nearby parked vehicle in order to get away from the beating he had sustained.

Mario had grabbed the boy's feet and had begun pulling him out from under the car as Andrew had continued to savagely beat the boy repeatedly with the buckle on the back, arms, head, feet, hands, and anywhere else that he could. Pancho stood in the same spot without moving and was trying to process the surreal, violent scene taking place before him. The effects of the drugs he had consumed and the drama unfolding before him made it all seem like a movie or a dream.

The boy had begun to plead for his very life. He had begun to beg for mercy for the beating to cease. But Andrew had kept swinging the buckle as hard as he could with extreme malice and intent.

Pancho had suddenly heard a door burst open from his girlfriend's house. A wild-eyed, beatnik-looking man holding a rifle in his hands poised and ready to fire had come running out and shouting for the boys to leave the illegal Mexican boy alone. Pancho and his two friends had glanced at the mad man and did not hesitate for one second to react. They knew that they had to run for their lives and leave that place immediately.

Pancho had yelled at the top of his lungs, "Run, run, run! We've got to get out of here or we are dead!"

All three boys instinctively and instantaneously had begun to run at high velocity. They had only taken three steps when one of the strangest things that had ever happened to Pancho occurred. Everything had turned into slow motion. Pancho, Andrew, and Mario had been running side by side, and elbow to elbow when a loud shot rang out.

Pancho was on the far left side, Andrew was in the middle, and Mario was on the right. The blast from the rifle had been deafening and had filled the cold night air like a cannon's flare. The boys must have been fifty feet away from the mad gunman when the shot had been fired. Pancho had looked at Andrew and Mario and was expecting to hear the bullet ricochet off of the pavement underneath their feet, but it didn't. Pancho had asked the boys if any of them had been hit. They both had answered and said, "No!"

This had all happened in a split second. Pancho knew that it did not take more than three seconds for a bullet to reach its target from fifty feet away. But time had been moving in slow motion at the moment for some reason. Pancho had attributed this to the drugs playing tricks on his mind. Whatever had been the cause, this particular sequence of events had actually happened.

As soon as Andrew and Mario had answered Pancho that they were not hit, Andrew stumbled. Pancho and Mario caught him and had kept on running. Andrew had begun to shout that he was hit. He had begun yelling that the bullet was burning him like as if molten lava had been poured on him, "It burns, it burns, it burns!"

Pancho knew all the streets in his neighborhood. He also knew all the back alleyways, all the hideouts, and escape routes that were used to get away from the police or an angry father of a girl he had tried to seduce. The staggering trio had been pursued by the gunman and they had been able to hear many more shots being fired in their direction. The gunman had been shouting obscenities at the boys and swearing that he would kill them if he caught up to them.

The boys had made their way to the first back alleyway they saw and had evaded the menacing gunman. They had been running in the dark and had felt the sweat oozing out of their bodies. They heard their heartbeats racing within their chests. Their mind had begun to plead and urge their feet to move faster because their life depended on it.

The boys had jumped two fences into someone's back yard. Pancho would go over the fence first. Mario would then carry Andrew up and over the fence and hand him to Pancho on the other side. They had finally come to the last fence that bordered Andrew's home. They stopped for a second to think about what had just transpired. Pancho had asked Andrew, "How are you doing?"

Andrew answered, "I'm okay, but the bullet burns like fire. Thanks for helping me get away from that crazy dude with the rifle."

The boys had only one fence to make it over and Andrew would be home safe. They took one deep breath and Pancho jumped the wooden fence and waited on the other side for Mario to heave Andrew over.

Once Andrew had been placed over, Mario hopped the fence and pulled Andrew's arm over his shoulder and Pancho did the same. With their arms intertwined around each other in order to support Andrew's weight, the trio had looked forward into the grassy lot and told each other, "We made it!"

They had all taken one step forward, but didn't realize that they had been standing on top of a small mound of dirt. They fell down face first into the ground. The trio could not believe that they had just fallen down. They were face down in the dirt with their arms around each other and they began to laugh uncontrollably. Even Andrew had begun to laugh in spite of the pain caused by the bullet wound.

They eventually made their way back to their feet and took Andrew to the front porch of his house. Pancho and Mario had made up their minds that they did not want to be around when Andrew's parents came to the door. They knocked on the door and had steadied Andrew so that he would not fall down. As soon as the porch light came on and the door had opened, Pancho and Mario ran away from the scene.

Pancho looked back and saw Andrew's dad catch him as he was about to fall to the ground. Andrew's dad was hysterical and was asking what had happened to him. Andrew told him that he had been shot. This was the last thing Pancho had heard as he fled the scene.

Pancho and Mario had made their way to Pancho's house which was located just down the block from Andrew's house. Pancho and his family lived at the last house on a dead end street named Kearney.

Andrew had not died. He had been hit on the calf and would probably have a slight limp for the rest of his life. All three boys had been charged with assault and were put on probation for one year. The mad gunman was never charged. Pancho was sure that the Mexican illegal teenage boy had died after the severe beating he sustained, but he didn't.

Pancho had seen him sitting on the porch of Joann's house, his ex-girlfriend, looking like a mummy. The Mexican boy had bandages all over his body, form head to toe. He had spent two weeks in the hospital recovering from his wounds. The poor boy will be scared for the rest of his life. And Pancho will never know why the boy hadn't simply said, "Hello."

❧ CHAPTER 6 ❧

THE TASMANIAN DEVIL

Pancho's older brother, Pistol Pete, had been planning to throw an immense and spirited party. Pistol Pete had wanted to celebrate the arrival of summer as well as his income tax return which he had doctored up quite nicely in his favor. His plans were to invite as many friends as he could. This was going to be a big, blow-out party!

The blissful activities for this festive bash would include a live local rock band, six 16-gallon kegs of Budweiser beer (iced down for some cold summer refreshment), barbecued chicken, sausages, *fajitas*, hallucinogenic mushrooms, LSD, and plenty of the best Mexican marijuana for the party attendees. The party had been set for Saturday night and the invitations had gone out.

The party had started at 6:00 P.M. The food had begun to be served and the first keg of beer had been popped opened. A good crowd had already shown up at this early hour because everyone loves free food and free beer. The sun had been high in the sky and had blasted its fiery rays on all the party-goers as they mingled in Pistol Pete's backyard.

Some of the people that had shown up included Fat Fêfê, Blonde-haired Mario, Benny-Low (he was called this because he walked with a swagger that gave him the appearance that he was low to the ground), Psycho Michael (he frequently acted in bizarre manners), and Stoner (always had Marijuana).

Others included Big Lou (a big man of six feet two inches; which is very big for a Hispanic), Cousin Mando (first cousin of Pancho), Leaping Lou (he was called this because he had long legs that made him look like a grasshopper that was ready to leap), and Wolf (he had abundant facial hair since he was twelve).

There had also been some beautiful girls present such as resplendent and elegant Gogi. This girl was the prettiest and sexiest teenager in town. She was suave and sophisticated. She was stylish and cool. She was cool just like lightening. She had the ability to make hundreds of teenage boys drool like Pavlov's Dogs with just a sway of her fully rounded hips. There was also Fancy Nancy (she was another splendiferous young female guitarist of the South Side that could bring thoughts of sweet desire to any boy), Kwi-Kwi (no one knows why she was called this, but she was a cool and pretty girl), and Sylvia Monreal (she had the elegant and sultry looks of Lauren Bacall; she could make young boys melt with a simple look).

There were also some of the trouble makers present such as Tattoo Eddie (he was called this because he was a home-made tattoo artist as well as having many tattoos all over his body), Head Hunter Eddie (he was called this because he would try to rip peoples heads off when playing full contact sports), Andrew (was walking around with a slight limp due to having been shot on the leg), Big Head Mike (he had a big head), Jabber Jaw Anthony (he had a resemblance to the cartoon shark), Cha Ching (was called this because he was always asking for money), Charles (was always ready and willing to fight), and of course, Pancho Martinez just to name a few.

Many other people had continued to pile into the backyard as nightfall began to creep in. There were people that had been invited by a friend of a friend of a friend. There were also some people that no one knew at all.

At sundown, the Rock Band *Wicked Step* (with a female drummer) began to perform its high volume, high intensity, and hard hitting hard rock music. The beer and illegal drugs had been flowing freely throughout the night. Everyone was having a good time and enjoying the party and not a single fight had broken out among the crowd; this in itself was a miracle.

Pancho Martinez had been unable to remove the illegal smile from his face no matter how hard he tried. And he had tried. He had found himself in the bathroom speaking to his reflection in a mirror trying to reason as to why his reflection should stop smiling so much. Of course, this had been due to the mixture of alcohol and LSD. His smile would have eventually gone away as soon as the affect of the drugs had worn off, but that wouldn't have been until the next morning.

The party had been a huge success. It went down in the history books of the beer drinkers and rebel rousers as one of the biggest and best illicit parties in the history of San Antonio's Southeast Side. At around 3:00 A.M., the last of the guests had made their way out of the backyard and left.

Pistol Pete had passed out due to the high consumption of alcohol. The night was still and solemn and the only person who was awake was Pancho Martinez with his illegal smile.

Pancho's heart was racing. His mind, will, and emotions were telling him to keep going. Going where, he did not know. All he knew was that his entire being was glad to be alive and experiencing the magnificence of the moment.

Pancho had quietly gone into the living room and sat next to a newly opened keg of beer. The keg was full and ice cold. There was no way that he could have left it alone. It would have gone against the religion of his drunken Mexican ancestors. So, Pancho sat down with a man-sized mug (twelve inches high with a mouth six inches in diameter) made out of clear glass that he had stolen from a carnival game booth during fiesta at the downtown Market Square.

He had filled the mug to the brim, then put on Moxy's debut album (the one with the black cover with only "Moxy" written on it) on the record player and proceeded to play the song *Moon Rider* (his favorite song at the time). He leaned back on the living room couch as he sat by himself. In Pancho Martinez's mind, it could not have been any better than this moment. He was at peace, had a cold glass of beer in his hands, and was listening to some great rock and roll.

When 4:00 A.M. had come around, Pancho Martinez was still reflecting and pondering the music and the moment when he heard a quiet knock at the front door. At first he thought he was hallucinating, but then he heard it again. He stopped the record player (which was now playing Budgie's *Napoleon Bonaparte*) to see if someone was indeed rapping at the door.

Hundreds of thoughts flooded his mind as to who was

at the door. His first thought had been that Gogi had come back to be with him in this serene and surreal moment to be the queen of all his dreams. Next, he thought that it was the police coming to arrest him for providing illegal drugs and alcohol to his friends. Maybe it was Charles or Stoner coming back to help him finish the last keg of beer?

Then his mind had gone blank. He could not figure out who was at the door. He had begun to panic in his bewilderment and confusion. Who would be knocking at the door at four in the morning? He then had become angry at the unidentified, but persistent knocker. How dare they disturb his pleasant trip? His smile had suddenly come back and had reminded him that everything was alright. Nothing or no one could have been able to ruin that extraordinary night. All he had to do was open the door and the mystery would be over.

Pancho Martinez had slowly walked to the door with calm and curiosity on his mind. He was calm because he was unafraid of whoever was at the door. He was curious because he felt stumped by this late-night riddle. He grabbed the door knob and slowly cracked the door open just enough to peek out with one eye. At first glance, Pancho thought he had seen the Tasmanian Devil; the cartoon character from the Bugs Bunny cartoons.

Was it the drugs? Was it the poor lighting on the front porch? Or was it really the Tasmanian Devil standing at the door? Pancho Martinez had closed his eyes and had shaken his head in an attempt to clear his vision and mind in order to refocus on the creature standing on the front porch. This time he opened the door wide enough to stick his head beyond the door frame in order to get a closer look. Now that his eyes had been focused, he could finally make out who was at the door. It was Tattoo Eddie.

Pancho Martinez did not know Tattoo Eddie well; he was more of an acquaintance and a closer friend to his brother, Pistol Pete. Tattoo Eddie stood at five feet zero inches. He was a very dark skinned Hispanic with thick, wavy, jet-black hair and a huge bulky mustache on his face. He had skinny legs, a very thin waist, and an extremely broad chest. All of these features made him look exactly like the Tasmanian Devil.

Not only did he resemble the cartoon character, but he also acted like him. Tattoo Eddie had great ferocity and rage and was well known for his cruelty and malice. He was one short, mean and ugly fiend that no one wanted to tangle with or dispute. Even Pancho Martinez had some reservation and apprehension in dealing with the Tasmanian Devil.

Pancho Martinez stood at the door and stared at Tattoo Eddie with bewilderment. He was baffled and wondered why in the world the Tasmanian Devil would be knocking at the door at four in the morning. "Hey, what's up dude? Everyone's asleep, what can I do for you?" exclaimed Pancho Martinez in a soft, quiet voice so that he would not have woken up anyone in the house.

Tattoo Eddie had this obscure look on his face and answered Pancho with, "Come on out here, I need to talk to you."

Pancho had thought this to be very out of the ordinary and there was no way he was going to go outside alone with the Tasmanian Devil. Pancho responded, "Pete's asleep, you'll have to come back later on in the day."

Tattoo Eddie asked him again to come outside. Pancho could not figure this out; why would the Tasmanian Devil want to speak with him, and why at 4:00 A.M.? As he pondered the Tasmanian Devil's proposal, he had glanced around and saw that an old, four door, pale blue, 1960's Chevrolet Impala sedan was parked in front of the house with four older Hispanic gentlemen sitting in it. "This must be the Tasmanian Devil's ride; and who knows who those four hombres are," Pancho thought to himself.

Then the Tasmanian Devil had asked again, "Why don't you come out here, so I can talk to you?"

Pancho was really apprehensive, but the alcohol was giving him a false sense of bravery that emboldened him. He had begun to sing to himself Tom Petty's *I Won't Back Down* song, "Hey baby, there ain't no easy way out. I'll stand my ground and I won't back down."

Pancho had stepped outside on the front porch and the Tasmanian Devil slowly backed up along the sidewalk that led toward the street and Pancho followed him. The Tasmanian Devil stopped and stared at Pancho in the face. Pancho asked, "So, what's up?"

Then, surprisingly, and completely unexpected, the Tasmanian Devil had swung his right fist and hit Pancho directly on his left eye. Pancho was stunned but did not go down to the floor because he was used to fighting and getting hit. Pancho knew that he was in for the fight of his life. He would have to gather all of the courage, strength, and vigor that lay deep inside of his Aztecan warrior and Pancho Villa Mexican marauder soul.

Pancho had put on his best boxing moves and threw a straight right cross that made the Tasmanian Devil duck down. Then Pancho gave him his best double left hook (one punch to the ribs and then another to the face) followed by a five-punch combination to the face. This would normally have floored the ordinary person on the streets, but it had not fazed his current adversary. It only infuriated Pancho's malicious foe.

The Tasmanian Devil had gone into a frenzy (much like the cartoon character) and had begun to swing and flail his fists repeatedly and wildly in a circular whirlwind motion toward Pancho. At first, Pancho had not known what to do to counter the attack from such a fanatical assailant. Then he had remembered a move that his brother Pistol Pete had used on a person twice his size and outweighed him by two hundred pounds – a flying football tackle to the chest.

Pancho had lunged forward in his best football tackling posture but tried to duck the forthcoming fists at the same time so he ended up tackling the Tasmanian's knees. Pancho had pushed and tugged as hard as he could at the Tasmanian Devil's knees but could not knock him down. If he could only have gotten the Tasmanian to the ground, then he could have pounded his fists into his face and beaten him into submission.

But the Tasmanian Devil was not about to go down. Pancho had returned to his feet and tried the maneuver again. Nothing happened. Pancho tried it a third time, but still nothing happened.

At that moment Pancho's eight-year-old nephew, Adam Rene, (Pistol Pete's eldest son) had come to the door and yelled at the Tasmanian Devil to leave his uncle alone. Pancho yelled at his nephew to go call his father for back up. The nephew had disappeared and returned with the bad news that he could not wake up his valiant and fearless, passed-out father. Meanwhile, Pancho and the Tasmanian Devil were exchanging blows in a close clinch.

Pancho had then told his nephew to go get a baseball bat or some form of weapon to help get the Tasmanian Devil off of him. Adam Rene returned with an old Louisville slugger that had often been used to attack stray dogs and drunken fools. Pancho ran to the door and grabbed the baseball bat and had begun to swing away. The Tasmanian Devil had begun to retreat in fright. He had begun to yell at the men in the car to open the door. The door was not opened by the time he reached the car, so he dove in through the window head first in order to avoid getting hit by the baseball bat.

He then had ordered the men to drive off as fast as they could, "This dude is crazy! Let's get out of here now before he starts breaking the windows!" The car had sped off with its wheels screeching and smoke billowing high into the dark night sky.

On the following day, Pistol Pete told Pancho that the Tasmanian Devil had come by his house in the morning around 10:00 A.M. to discuss the previous night's hostilities. Pancho had a huge shiner on his left eye and some bumps and bruises on his head and shoulders. Pistol Pete told Pancho, "You should have seen the Tasmanian Devil. He had two black eyes, his face was swollen, and both his lips had been busted."

Pancho Martinez had taken on the Tasmanian Devil in an all-out fist fight and won. Not many people could claim that accolade. Pancho was still wondering why this altercation had happened in the first place. Had he said or done something to the Tasmanian Devil during the party to instigate the fight? Pistol Pete said, "That's why he came by the house in the morning; to explain why he had instigated the brawl."

The Tasmanian Devil had been very apologetic for having gone to Pistol Pete's house and having started a fight, especially a fight with his brother. Earlier that day the Tasmanian Devil had stolen four ounces of Marijuana from those men that had been in the parked car. Those men were old-time drug dealers and had gone looking for the Tasmanian Devil in order to retrieve their Marijuana. The Tasmanian Devil had come up with the story that he had sold it to someone at the party and was waiting for the payment. The men did not care about that; they only wanted to get their weed back. This is why they had taken the Tasmanian Devil back to the party, so he could get their weed back for them.

The Tasmanian Devil had put himself in a bind. He didn't know if anyone would still have been at the party. He was hoping someone could help him to get out of the dangerous predicament he had put himself in. He was still making up the story when they arrived at the house. When Pancho had opened the door, the Tasmanian Devil thought he could use him as a patsy and say that he was the one that had the weed.

The Tasmanian Devil knew that Pancho was Pistol Pete's brother, but he hadn't known that Pancho could defend himself with such proficiency. The Tasmanian Devil told the men that he had hit Pancho because he had not wanted to give the weed back to him. After Pancho had gone crazy with the bat, the Tasmanian Devil told the men that Pancho was one mean dude and that they should not mess with him. The men had decided to make a deal with the Tasmanian Devil and said that they would forget about the weed if he would give them each a free tattoo. Of course, the Tasmanian Devil agreed.

One year later Pancho had been waiting for the bus in downtown San Antonio. He was standing at the corner of Houston and St. Mary's street across from the old Texas theatre building and the Gunter Hotel. He had been minding his own business and looking at all the pretty Hispanic girls walking by on the sidewalk. Suddenly, he noticed a commotion going on down the street near the Majestic theatre.

The sidewalks were filled people walking, shopping, and site-seeing. Pancho had noticed that the crowds were being pushed aside by someone or something that was making its way through the sidewalk. Old ladies were screaming, young girls were hissing and heckling, and some men were cursing and cussing as they were being pushed aside. Pancho had thought to himself, "Who could be so mean and calloused to push people around only to make a path for their walk way? Who could . . . ." Pancho had caught himself in mid sentence when he saw the familiar form of the Tasmanian Devil.

No one could have stood a chance when this guy was around; little old ladies, babies, people with special needs, or little girls they were all fair game for the Tasmanian Devil. Pancho had wondered if the Tasmanian Devil would notice him. Would he make his way toward Pancho to continue the previous fight from a year ago? And if so, how would Pancho react?

This was downtown San Antonio after all, and this was no place to act like a bunch of middle school kids out on the school playground. Pancho had pondered, "Should I stand my ground and fight again? Or would it be wiser to run away like a skinny wide receiver being chased by a six foot five, two-hundred-and-fifty-pound middle linebacker after a short-completed pass?" Pancho looked down the sidewalk and had noticed that the Tasmanian Devil was getting closer.

Pancho stiffened up and had begun to attempt to gather his courage (he would need it if the Tasmanian Devil noticed him). The Tasmanian Devil was now a few feet away from him. Pancho had bit into his bottom lip and looked straight ahead in front of him and did not turn to the left or to the right. He was hoping that if he did not make eye contact with the Tasmanian Devil he would not be noticed. But his plan did not work.

The Tasmanian Devil had walked right up to Pancho and stood squarely in front of him. He had inched his way closer and closer toward Pancho until their faces were centimeters apart. Pancho had said nothing. He just stood there frozen in time and space. The Tasmanian Devil looked at Pancho in the eyes, smiled, and then walked away without saying a word.

Pancho hadn't seen or heard about the Tasmanian Devil after that day until he read an article in the *San Antonio Express News* newspaper. The story was about two young men walking down *Chihuahua* Street in the West Side of San Antonio. One of the men was the Tasmanian Devil. A huge, ferocious pit bull had run across from an alley and attacked the second man. Tattoo Eddie had grabbed a two-by-four that was lying nearby and beat the dog to death and saved his friend's life.

A reporter from the Express News had interviewed Tattoo Eddie for the heroic act of saving his friend's life. The reporter ran the story on the front page and the headline read: **"Spurs Fan Saves Friend's Life from a Ferocious Pit Bull!"** Tattoo Eddie called the reporter and said, "I'm not a Spurs fan!"

The reporter responded, "Well, I just thought that since you are from San Antonio that you would be a Spurs fan. I'll correct the mistake in tomorrow's paper."

The next day the front page read: **"Silver Stars Fan Saves Friend's Life from a Ferocious Pit Bull!"** Tattoo Eddie called the reporter and protested, "I'm not a Silver Stars fan either!"

The frustrated reporter had asked the irritated Tattoo Eddie, "Are you a basketball fan at all?"

Tattoo Eddie had happily responded, "Yes. As a matter of fact, I am a die-hard Los Angeles Lakers fan." The reporter had agreed to make the change in the next day's newspaper. The next day the front page read: **"Tasmanian Devil Wannabe Kills Beloved Family Pet!"**

❧ CHAPTER 7 ❧

THE WHITE SHOES INCIDENT

The magnificent festival of "Fiesta" in San Antonio has taken place every April to honor the memory of the heroes of the Alamo, the Battle of San Jacinto, and to celebrate San Antonio's rich and diverse cultures. In 1891, a group of ladies decorated horse-drawn carriages, paraded in front of the Alamo, and bombarded each other with flower blossoms. Thus, the "Battle of Flowers Parade" was born and has become an annual event that has grown into a multi-cultural community celebration unlike any other in the United States.

"Fiesta San Antonio" has grown into an elaborate ten-day citywide celebration. It has featured more than one hundred events including a carnival, balls and coronations, music, food, sports, pageantry, exhibits, parades, and military and patriotic observances. The "St. Mary's Oyster Bake" has also been a part of this festival. The Oyster Bake has included two days of food and fun plus tens of thousand of oysters and live music on the St. Mary's University campus. Millions of people have attended from all around the world.

There have been more than 75,000 volunteers at the events, and millions of dollars that have greatly impacted the San Antonio economy.

Pancho Martinez and his family had been attending Fiesta every year ever since he could remember. It had truly been a family affair that included aunts, uncles, cousins, nieces and nephews that would gather yearly for the momentous occasion. The adults would take advantage of the festival to have an all-out drunken beer bash. The kids seized upon the fun, excitement, and clamor with their siblings and other extended family members in a public setting.

When Pancho was in his late teens he would get totally wasted at the "Fiesta" festivities just like his parents and relatives did. He would begin drinking early in the afternoon and by nightfall he was ready to pass out like a clumsy Humpty-Dumpty. He and his thug friends would all go together to look for Mexican cuties that were in abundance at "Fiesta" in all shapes and sizes.

One of Pancho's favorite lines that he had when he met a young cutie for the first time was, "How about a kiss?"

To his surprise, the majority of the girls would all say yes and give him a great big kiss on the lips. Pancho was a particularly good kisser. He had known this because every girl that he had kissed was very impressed with his exceptional talent. Maybe it was due to his full robust lips? Or maybe it was due to the fact that he got an early start as a kisser?

When Pancho was four years old he had partaken in his first French kissing session. His brother Pistol Pete, who was eight years older than Pancho, had many beautiful girlfriends flocking around him. One girl in particular, Sue Ann, who was sixteen years old and the epitome of a beautiful Cherokee princess, was Pistol Pete's favorite. Sue Ann had long, straight, black hair down to her waist, smooth as silk light-brown skin, high cheek bones, a straight and narrow nose, a great body with all her muscles well defined, and the prettiest and friendliest smile in the world.

On one particular day when Pancho's parents were not at home, Pistol Pete had some of his buddies over for some company. They were in the living room watching TV. Pistol Pete and Sue Ann were having a heavy make-out session on the old lime green love seat that did not match any of the other furniture in the living room. Young Pancho walked into the living room and had noticed the smooching couple's intense attention to each other's mouths.

Pancho had never seen anything like this in his short life. He planted himself directly in front of the couple and proceeded to analyze the situation. Pistol Pete had noticed his younger sibling staring at them, so he stopped kissing Sue Ann and asked, "Why are you staring at us?"

Pancho answered with innocent and simplistic curiosity, "Why are you sticking your tongues down each other's throat?"

Pistol Pete and Sue Ann began to laugh uncontrollably at Pancho's question. "We are French kissing. Haven't you ever heard of a French Kiss?" said Pistol Pete.

Pancho had never heard of this. The only kiss he knew about was kissing his mother or his aunts pinching and kissing his cheeks during the holidays. Pistol Pete then did something that Pancho will never forget, he told Sue Ann to show Pancho how to give and receive a French kiss. Sue

Ann willingly and without hesitation sat Pancho down on the love seat and proceeded to demonstrate the workings of a French kiss inside of Pancho's mouth.

Pancho had immediately caught on to the intricate techniques and thoroughly enjoyed the private lesson. Ever since then Pancho has been wowing girls with his passionate melt-in-your-mouth, curl your toes, and make you stutter certified kisses.

Every year during "Fiesta" Pancho would end up in the local Bexar county jail for public intoxication or disturbing the peace. He would spend the night in the "Drunk Tank," a large holding room where all the inebriated, disorderly and unruly morons would be placed to cool off and sober up. Then they'd be let out the following morning to go home or continue their drunken revelry and repeat the vicious cycle all over again.

On one particular year, the two weeks of "Fiesta" had taken a turn for the worse. On the first week of "Fiesta" Pancho, his brothers Pistol Pete and Dealing Dave (who had just gotten out of the army after four years in the Eighty-Second Airborne Division), his cousins Mando, Ronnie, and Tudy, were walking the grounds at the carnival festivities. They had been drinking beer, looking for girls, and laughing at and making fun of the people in the crowds.

They were all adept at making fun of people. And there were many easy targets to insult at the carnival. There were people with big ears, big noses, and big feet. There were girls with their unsightly bellies hanging out of their blouses. There were girls in clothes two sizes too small for them, and guys wearing the most mismatched clothes this side of a circus.

The boys had been having a blast and enjoying the cool April night breeze when they came to a dart booth game where the person in charge was a very peculiar looking woman. She had wild, dirty-blonde, matted hair just passed her shoulders. She only had one front tooth in her head. She had one crooked eye brow that went all the way across her forehead. And she had an ugly homemade tattoo on her left arm that read, "White Trash."

She was definitely no beauty queen. Dealing Dave had immediately gone up to her and had begun to launch insults at her. The woman was caught off guard and did not know what had hit her. Dealing Dave snapped, "You are so ugly that your face could cure rabies. Your nose is so big that you give Pinocchio a bad name. People must call you "bottle opener" with that one front tooth you got there." The dart game woman was infuriated and had begun to use profanity in her defense, but Dealing Dave just kept on dishing out the insults.

Pancho and the others stood stunned and could not believe Dealing Dave's brazenness with this woman that he had never met. Suddenly, the dart game woman had jumped on top of the booth counter. She continued to shout with great fervor at Dealing Dave and waved her forefinger in his face. But Dealing Dave just kept on with his banter.

The dart game woman was beside herself and had become engulfed in a great rage at this point. She reached over and grabbed a dart from the game board on the wall and thrust it with great force at Dealing Dave. A huge crowd had gathered by this time and everyone in the crowd, including Pancho ducked and then gasped at the dart game woman's "Chinese Connection-like" action.

The dart had landed and imbedded itself on Dealing Dave's left arm. Dealing Dave stood frozen with disbelief. She then grabbed a second dart and threw it at Dealing Dave, then a third, and a fourth. The darts had landed on Dealing Dave and stuck there protruding from his chest.

Dealing Dave had instinctively pulled out all four of the darts and began to throw them back at the dart game woman. She began yelling and screaming for help as the darts hit their mark on her back and arms. The police quickly arrived and arrested Dealing Dave for assaulting the dart game woman and for public intoxication.

Pancho, Pistol Pete and their cousins had walked away quietly from the scene to avoid being implicated in the affair. The charges were dropped against Dealing Dave and he was released the following morning with four dart wounds, a huge hangover, and a new-found respect for women with one tooth in their heads.

The following week, on Saturday night after the "Flambeau" night parade, Pancho found himself again at the carnival festivities. This was usually the highest attended night of "Fiesta." There were so many people that a person could hardly walk down the streets where the carnival games and food booths were set up. People were literally face-to-face, and it could take thirty minutes to travel a distance of fifty feet.

Pancho had started drinking beer early in the afternoon and by nightfall he was so drunk that he could hardly stand. He had attended the night parade with his buddies but had lost them in the crowd as the thousands in attendance at the parade rushed to the carnival area. He had found himself alone and unable to walk without stumbling, his speech was severely slurred, and his usual prowess had left him several beers ago.

He was trying to be smooth and suave in order to meet some beautiful girls to flirt with, but his situation wasn't allowing him to be at his best. He found a lamp post to lean against, but even this could not keep him from swaggering like an out of control helicopter. He was continually spilling beer from a plastic carnival cup on many of the passers-by. He was also trying to coarsely grope any girl that passed within striking distance.

It didn't take long before complaints from many disgruntled females had reached some police officers. The police immediately made their way toward Pancho and found him harassing and trying to get a kiss from a young, blonde tourist from Logan's Port, Indiana. The police grabbed Pancho and slammed him face down into the sidewalk. They slapped on the hand cuffs and began to read him his rights. Pancho didn't even see what hit him.

Pancho was puckering up to get the sweetest kiss from a hot young girl, the next thing he knew he was being wrestled down to the ground by four San Antonio police officers dressed in blue. "Wait," exclaimed Pancho, "Let me kiss this cute white girl from Indian Port, wherever that is, before you take me."

The police had rushed Pancho to a nearby "paddy wagon" that was standing by for just such a person, to escort them to jail. There were ten other men in the vehicle when Pancho was thrown in. After forty-five minutes of sitting in the vehicle they finally made their way toward the notorious Bexar County Jail.

Upon arrival at the jail, which was only one hundred

yards away from the carnival, Pancho was booked and sent to the "Drunk Tank" to sober up and cool off. The "Drunk Tank" was set up to hold thirty people, but on this night, there were nearly one hundred foul smelling men crowded into the holding room. There were people standing, sitting, lying down, sleeping, passed out, and crying. Some had been mouthing off to the guards and others were mouthing off to anybody that would listen.

Pancho just picked a corner in the room, sat down on the floor, and tried to get some sleep. He knew it was going to be a long, tiring night. As he tried to get some rest, he could hear some commotion from the other men in the room and would periodically look up to make sure no one was trying to sneak up on him and brutally attack him. That sort of thing was normal in the Bexar County jail.

Pancho had overheard three illegal alien Mexicans that must have been in their early twenties conferring diligently over something that was not too clear to him. One of the men was wearing a dingy white t-shirt with some tattered blue jeans that did not fit him well at all. He had an obtruding scar on his upper lip that must have been put there to poorly repair a cleft lip. Pancho mentally dubbed him, "Scar Lip."

Another man had a pink plaid dress shirt that was tucked very tightly and snuggly into his polyester mustard yellow pants. He had a very large square head with an apparent five-inch jagged scar on the side of his head that began on his forehead and trailed down to his cheek. The scar was rough and serrated and about one inch wide. Pancho mentally dubbed him, "Frankenstein."

The other man was thin, tall, and dressed in mismatched western clothes with orange pointy boots. His head was tilted to the side and he could not straighten it out. He was evidently born with this orthopedic defect. Pancho mentally dubbed him, "Side Winder."

Pancho had tried to concentrate on their conversation and heard Scar Lip tell the others, "Did you see that guy over there with the white shoes?"

Frankenstein answered and said, "Yeah, look at him, he thinks he looks real cool with his fancy clothes and fancy white shoes."

Some young Hispanic guy had been passed out on his back on a bench that was centered in the middle of the room. The guy was fully dressed in a fancy disco outfit with a lavender, silk shirt; black, bell bottom, polyester pants; a long, dangling, white scarf; and of course, a pair of shiny, patent leather, white dress shoes. Pancho had looked over with one eye opened at the disco enthusiast that was lying on his back and let out a hardy chuckle that he tried to hide in order to remain inconspicuous among the crowd.

The three illegal Mexicans had begun to get louder and continued to ridicule the disco enthusiast in order to attract attention toward themselves. "Check him out, do you think his mother helped to get him dressed?" sneered Scar Lip.

"No, I don't think so," answered Frankenstein, "No one's mother could be that dumb."

Side Winder chimed in, "Why don't we go over and steal his shoes? How much do you think we can get for them?"

Pancho had been trying to ignore the noisy trio. But now the stakes were being raised by the Mexicans engaging the sleeping numbskull with white shoes.

Pancho had told himself that this was none of his

business and that he would not get involved. He wasn't even going to bother looking up to see the confrontation occur. Just then, the three illegal Mexicans had drummed up the courage and talked themselves into going over and apprehending the glossy white shoes.

Pancho heard them say, "If he wakes up, we'll beat the tar out of him and still take his shoes."

Curiosity had gotten the best of Pancho. He was not able to resist looking up to see what was about to occur. Maybe there would be a fight? He wouldn't mind watching a good fight at the moment. Pancho had seen the three illegal Mexicans get up and commenced to circle the disco enthusiast. Pancho looked around to see if anyone was going to warn or help the passed out disco enthusiast.

Everyone in the tank was looking at the illegal Mexicans with curiosity and no one had any intentions of helping anybody. In fact, some of occupants were spurring on the daring trio. Pancho then looked at the disco enthusiast to see if he knew what was about to happen to him, but the sleeping disco dancer didn't even have a clue.

Pancho had been unable to see the disco enthusiast's face from his vantage point. All he was able to see were those white shoes. Pancho had straightened out his back and rose up a bit to see if he could get a glimpse of the disco dancer's face. The three illegal Mexicans were in place and had begun to whoop and holler and raise their arms in the air as they prepared to steal the white shoes. Pancho had looked again at the disco dancer to try and make out his face. "Wait a minute," Pancho told himself, "This disco dancer looks familiar!"

He had focused again on the disco dancer and his

mouth fell open in disbelief. He had in fact recognized the sleeping disco dancer! It was his brother Dealing Dave!

Pancho had been faced with a difficult predicament. Should he mind his own business? Or should he defend his comatose, drunk, disco dancing brother? Of course, he wanted to defend his brother, but the odds were stacked against him: three illegal Mexicans against one tired hero defending white shoes. Why not let them take the white shoes? Why not relax, rest, and laugh about it tomorrow? No, he was not about to do that. It was the principle of the matter: no one messes with your family!

Pancho had stood up and stretched his arms, legs, and back and began to move toward the illegal Mexicans, "Hey, slow down there and back up" he yelled out.

The three illegal Mexicans were stunned, as well as everyone else in the cell. Everyone had thought they were going to be in for some cheap entertainment at the disco dancer's expense and no one expected someone to stand up and dissuade the illegal Mexicans.

"Hey, mind your own business, sit back down and get out of our way, or you'll get hurt!" answered the Mexicans.

Pancho responded, "You don't know who I am, and you don't want to mess with me. So just calm down, back off and sit down!"

Scar Lip answered, "What is this to you? You better sit down, or we will really hurt you!"

Pancho had looked at everyone in the room and spoke loudly so that everyone would hear him well, "My name is Pancho Martinez! That's my brother lying there in the white shoes! Nobody messes with him!"

Pancho was not about to argue or discuss the matter

further with the illegal Mexicans, this was not his style. If someone had a disagreement or quarrel with him, he would settle it with his fists. He quickly moved to attack the trio by using the element of surprise. They would not be expecting him to suddenly pounce on them.

He punched Scar Lip on the face with a straight right hand, kicked Frankenstein in the groin, then grabbed Side Winder by the throat with his left hand and rapidly hit him in the eye with three successive right hands. There was blood splashing everywhere in the room as teeth and flesh flew in the air. The Mexicans began to yell hysterically like scared little girls on an amusement park ride.

By the time Pancho released Side Winder, Scar Lip had recovered his senses enough to lunge on top of Pancho and commence an unsteady attempt at a take down. Pancho had put him in a head lock and had begun to squeeze the life out of him as his eyes bulged out of his head. Then Frankenstein and Side Winder jumped on top of Pancho and had begun to swing their fists wildly at Pancho. Some of the wild shots were connecting Pancho on the face, arms and chest, but were not causing any major damage. Pancho had to get them off of him and subdue them before things got out of hand and he would end up on the losing end of this predicament.

Everyone in the tank and some guards that had gathered to view the fight were yelling excitedly for the action to continue. Pancho quickly gave Frankenstein his best Bruce Lee karate chop to the throat which sent the Mexican down to the ground gasping for air. He punched Side Winder on the thigh repeatedly until he also went down to the floor in agony. Pancho then threw Scar Lip against the cell bars and commenced to pummel him with his fists. The Mexican went limp and was out cold.

Pancho stood up and looked at all the other inmates and said, "My name is Pancho Martinez! That's my brother lying there with the white shoes! No one messes with him!" Pancho had walked calmly back to his corner and sat down with his knees up so that he could rest his head upon them and try to get some sleep. He looked up at Dealing Dave and noticed that he was sound asleep and had not been aware of the entire incident.

Six hours later a guard had called out Dealing Dave's name and told him he was going home. Dealing Dave got up, white shoes and all, and left the cell and never noticed Pancho sitting in the corner.

✹ CHAPTER 8 ✺

WHO ARE YOU WITH?

The scene was a dreary, cigarette-smoke filled, southside Saturday night, hole-in-the-wall barroom which was almost empty. There was an over-weight barmaid who was friendly, but very lonely. She was standing behind the bar cleaning a drinking glass with a musty wash towel while Jimi Hendrix's "Hey Joe" played in the background. There were also three couples present: Beto and Ginger, a husband and wife elderly couple who argued a lot; Rick and Dulce, a younger couple consisting of a good-looking, stuck-up wife and overbearing husband; Frank and Marty, two dudes who were not gay, and were only looking for girls to pick up.

Ginger suddenly had begun to nag at her husband, "I knew I should have listened to my mother and not married a loser like you. Look at where we are on a Saturday night, in a hole-in-the-wall barroom. Couldn't you have gotten a job where you could have made some decent money? Why couldn't I have married a lawyer or a doctor? Instead, I had to marry a third-rate musician."

Her husband Beto responded to her, "I wish you had

married a lawyer or a doctor; then you wouldn't be married to me. All you ever do is complain, nag, and argue like a lawyer. And maybe a doctor could help you with your *arroz con pollo* thighs, your double chin, and your crooked eyebrows."

Dulce, with her big hair and masses of makeup on her double chinned face, had begun to brag to her husband, "Thank God that I had my hair and nails done today. I would never be caught dead in a place like this without my hair and nails done. I'd rather stick needles in my eyes than walk around looking like some of the women who come into this joint."

Her husband Rick answered her, "Why don't you just shut up before I slap you in front of all these people? I can never go anywhere without you going off like a drunken country queen."

Dulce was quick to respond with a smart aleck reply, "Don't you dare talk to me like that you prune-faced moron!"

Rick picked up his beer glass, which was full, and slammed it down on the table in disgust and in the process splashed its contents all over his wife's face. Rick exclaimed to his wife, "Look, I told you to shut up! What does a guy have to do to have a nice quiet drink on a Saturday night?"

Frank and Marty had been watching and studying the two couple's every move. Frank said to Marty, "Which one of them chicks would you take home with you?"

Marty responded, "I don't know? The one with the big hair is pretty, but she's kind of skinny. I like my women with some meat on them."

Frank asked, "What about the other one?" Marty responded, "That chick is ugly man. She's so ugly that one look at her on an early Sunday morning will give you a hangover so bad that not even big red and menudo could cure."

Frank answered Marty's uncouth remark by saying, "She's not that ugly. Do you want to know what ugly is? My ex-mother-in-law is ugly. When God was passing out good looks, she was out to lunch. She's so ugly that *Raid* puts her picture on each can of their product to kill roaches and small rodents."

Pancho Martinez had walked into the bar room looking so dandy and so fine. He walked up to the bar and the chubby barmaid and ordered a drink. "Bourbon and coke, Jack Daniels," requested Pancho.

Something seemed peculiar on this night with the sharp dressed *catrin*. He appeared to have a downcast demeanor upon his countenance. The barmaid, who had just handed Pancho his drink, began to inquire of Pancho, "Hey man, you're new around here. I don't know who you are, but you're kind of cute. What brings you around here? Why do you look so down?"

Pancho ignored her and just sat there like he never heard a sound and kept drinking his drink. The barmaid laughed nervously but was not bothered by his disregard of her because she was used to that type of treatment. "I don't mean to bother you," she commented. "I know that I'm no beauty queen, but if there is one thing that I do well, it's listening."

After an awkward moment of silence, Pancho took his drink in his hand, raised it to his lips, took a couple of sips, then looked up at the pleasantly plump barmaid and proceeded with his best impersonation of Tony Montana from the movie *Scar face*, "You want to know who I am. You really want to know who I am. Well let me tell you."

He stood up from the barstool and kicked it back with his right foot sending it screeching across the hoary wooden floor. He cleared his throat. He stuck his chest out with pride and arrogance like a satin peacock displaying his feathers. He stretched out both arms and exclaimed in a loud, clear voice, "I'm the Helter Skelter Psycho your mother warned you about! I'm the stranger who gives candy to little girls! I'm the mother-raper, father-stabber, high on laughing grass and firewater Mexican spitfire! I'm the mescaline madman looking for a fight on a Saturday night! I am the rooster-footed devil at the dance! I am the grandson of Johnny Durango! My name is Pancho Martinez and I'm the meanest, venomous dog that has ever lived! I just got out of the Bexar County jail and found out that my *amor consentida* is living with my ex-best friend Mike, or psycho, as I know him. I'm not having a good day at all, so I wish that everyone would just leave me alone!"

"I wish . . . . ." Pancho had paused for a brief moment to gather his thoughts, and then exploded with fury in an extreme manner. He had begun to overturn tables and kick chairs around the room like he was a cyclone on a rampage. Once he had knocked over all the tables and chairs that didn't have any people in them, he stood still for a moment to catch his breath and fix his hair. Pancho looked around the room and stared deeply into everyone's frightened eyes.

He then slowly and deliberately had begun to walk up to Rick who was nervously twitching at all the commotion caused by Pancho. He stood directly in front of Rick and grabbed him by his shirt collar with both of his hands and picked him up to his feet and yelled at him, "You better listen to what I have to say to you, and you better listen well. Whose side are you on? Who are you with, man? Tell me! Who are you with? Who are you with?"

Rick was trembling with fright, and he was sweating. All the blood had rushed away from his head, his knees buckled, and he was about to pass out. Pancho shook him feverishly by the throat and said, "Who are you with?"

The scared fellow could scarcely get a word out but gave it his best college try and stuttered out these words, "Man, I'm with you; whatever you say; I'm with you!"

Rick's wife Dulce, sarcastically cried out, "What are you afraid of? Why don't you talk to him the way you talk to me? I thought you were tough. What has happened to you?"

Beto and Ginger quickly and sheepishly chimed in unison, "We're with you too!"

Pancho had let go of Rick and walked away with repugnance and indifference upon his face. He took a seat at the bar and spoke to the barmaid, "I wish everyone would just leave me alone. Don't you ever wish for anything?"

The barmaid had been caught off guard by his question, not only because she was in shock at what had just transpired, but also because no one had ever bothered to inquire about her opinions, aspirations, or her dreams. The barmaid, however, had not hesitated to answer Pancho because she was afraid that he might change his mind and tell her to forget about sharing her thoughts with him.

She had let out a sad sigh and said, "I wish that I was beautiful; I wish I weren't so dog gone fat; I wish that you would notice me."

Pancho looked at her and had thought of what to say, but

no words were coming to mind. No songs were ringing in his head. Then he got a revelation from Bob Dylan and said, "I'm not the one you want babe; I'm not the one you need. You're looking for someone who's never weak, but always strong; someone who'll protect you and defend you whether you are right or wrong; someone to open each and every door, but it ain't me babe, it ain't me you're looking for."

Pancho had seen the sorrow and melancholy on the barmaid's face. It was real and deep. It penetrated down to her joints and marrow and infiltrated her soul and spirit.

Pancho was disappointed with himself for the portrayal of unscrupulous emotion he had just demonstrated by swarming and breaking the entire barroom floor. He was angered at the thought of his lovely dove in the arms of Psycho. He was also incensed at the betrayal of his once close friend. He had to vent his anger. Breaking things and beating people up was how he had been raised. This was how things were fixed on the streets. If there was a problem, it was fixed by beating someone's brains out.

He had noticed the barmaid's eyes beginning to tear up. He had already made a fool of himself, but he didn't want to be an insensitive fool. He searched for the appropriate words to console the unfortunate barmaid, "I ain't saying you ain't pretty. All I'm saying is I'm not ready for any person place or thing to try and pull the reins in on me." This was a quote from Linda Ronstadt's song "Different Drum."

The barmaid answered him, "But if you only give me a chance, you'd see that I'm a good person. I have a big heart and I have a lot to offer. Just give me one chance."

Pancho had begun to feel sympathy for the barmaid so he decided to speak from the heart instead of quoting a song.

He told her, "You don't want to get involved with me. I'm a mess. My life is a mess. I'm all mixed up. I'm searching for happiness and fulfillment in life, but I can't seem to find it. I feel a deep emptiness inside of me, but I don't know how to fill it. You don't want to fall in love with someone like me. You see, I don't even love myself."

❧ CHAPTER 9 ❧

THE UNLUCKIEST MAN IN SAN ANTONIO

Pancho Martinez had many friends and many more acquaintances. One such acquaintance was a guy by the name of Fernando. Fernando was a slightly plump, jovial, simple-minded guy who followed people around like a lost puppy. He had done so many drugs and sniffed so much spray paint in his young life that by the time he was in his early twenties his mental capabilities were very much diminished.

Fernando had been in and out of jail for most of his life and he even did a three year stretch at Huntsville prison. Life had not been kind to Fernando. He always got the short end of the stick in all situations. One day he decided that he was tired of the inconsideration in his life and tired of playing the role of a fool. He knew that he had done a lot of bad things in his life, a lot of things that he was really ashamed of, so he decided that suicide would be his ticket out.

He gathered up the little bit of valor that he had left and

decided to kill himself by electrocution. He had seen this done in an old Perry Mason show. He went to his mother's house. He went into the bathroom and filled the bathtub to the top. He got completely naked and sat down in it. He then retrieved a radio boom box and plugged it into a nearby outlet. He steadied his nerves and said his last goodbye to this cruel world and dropped the radio into the tub.

Sparks and smoke filled the entire bathroom. When Fernando had opened his eyes, he realized that nothing had happened to him. He was not dead or burned up. The only things that happened were that the radio was fried, and he blew all the fuses in the house.

His mother was furious when she found out what he had done. Not particularly because he had tried to commit suicide, but because he had ruined her best radio and blew out all the fuses. "What's wrong with you, you idiot? Don't you know that I spent a lot of money on that radio at Wal-Mart? And why did you blow all the fuses? Don't you know that you could have burned the house down?" she exclaimed as she slapped him on the side of his head repeatedly. Fernando reluctantly had to come up with another plan in order to do himself in.

Fernando decided to hang himself. He went to his mother's attic, which was so spacious that a person could walk upright in it very comfortably. He tied a rope to a huge crossbeam. He then stood up on a chair, tied a noose at the other end of the rope, put it snugly around his neck, and released the slack in the rope. He was certain that this would do the trick. He steadied his nerves and said his last goodbye to this cruel world and kicked the chair from under him.

As he dangled in the air, he told himself, "Man, this really hurts. I should have thought of another way to kill myself."

After two minutes of kicking, scratching, spitting, and several other bodily functions, the rope broke, and Fernando fell to the floor in a hard thud. He was not dead, just in a lot of pain. His plan had backfired again. He ended up with a sore throat and a cough for a week. The rope had cut into his neck so deep that it left a permanent scar around his neck that he will have to wear for the rest of his life. Fernando had to come up with yet another plan.

This time Fernando decided that he would kill himself by swallowing an entire bottle of pills. He went to his mother's medicine cabinet and grabbed the first five bottles of pills that he saw. He opened each one to examine the potential deadly pills. The first bottle had tiny pink pills that made Fernando think, "These are sissy pills and will probably make me smile a lot and want to dance to Broadway tunes." Those would not do the trick.

The second bottle had some small round yellow pills with the word "Valium" written on them. These pills didn't look deadly either, because how could something that made you get louder kill you, he thought? Fernando read the labels on the other bottles and they had such names as Lithium, Prozac, Thorazine, and *Cascara Sagrada*. Lithium sounded like helium and he didn't think that helium, a gas used to blow up balloons, could kill a person so that one wouldn't work. He had never heard of Prozac so that one wouldn't work. He had heard of Thorazine once in a song called the "Thorazine shuffle," but this was obviously another drug that made you want to dance. Cascara Sagrada, however, sounded menacing. This sounded like it could kill one hundred men with one pill.

So, Fernando steadied his nerves and said his last goodbye to this cruel world and swallowed the entire bottle. About twenty minutes later he had begun to get a severe stomach ache then he passed out. When he woke up, he found himself in the hospital connected to all kinds of tubes. The doctors informed him that they had to pump his stomach out because he had taken an entire bottle of a high strength laxative. Fernando was sore all over his body. His mouth and throat had hurt, his stomach hurt, and his head was pounding with a huge headache. Fernando told himself that this had not turned out to be such a good idea after all.

When Fernando had been released from the hospital, he decided that he would once and for all complete the task of killing himself by obtaining a gun and shooting himself in the head. This would certainly be deadly, and it would also be quick and painless.

He went to his mother's house and retrieved a handgun that his brother kept in the house for protection. The gun was a black, twenty-five caliber semi-automatic handgun. He went to his room and locked the door. He steadied his nerves and said his last goodbye to this cruel world. He raised the handgun to his right temple and pulled the trigger. When he woke up, he found himself at the Santa Rosa hospital with bandages around his head and another stupendous headache.

The doctors told him that a twenty-five-caliber handgun was not that powerful, and it also has a small bullet and thus did not cause any major damage. When Fernando fired the gun, the bullet penetrated his skin and lodged itself in his skull. They were able to retrieve the bullet quite easily.

A few days later when Fernando was released from the hospital, he ran into Pancho Martinez at Roosevelt Park. He told Pancho about the saga of his adventures in trying to kill himself. "I'm a miracle!" exclaimed Fernando. "I tried to kill myself over and over, but God did not want me to die just yet. Do you think God has a special plan for me?"

Pancho was astonished at Fernando's story, and he did believe that there was a reason that Fernando was still alive. God did have a plan for Fernando, but only God knew what that was going to be. Fernando will always have the burn marks on his body, the scar on his neck, and the hole in his head as a testimony of how God intervened in his life.

Fernando had many mishaps in his life, but it paled in comparison to the story of Benny Low. Benny's story was so captivating that the *San Antonio Express News* wrote about it one hot and blistering summer. The headline read, **"The Unluckiest Man in San Antonio!"**

Benny Low's story started at a local southside Handy Andy grocery store on St. Mary's street near the King William area. Charles and Benny were hanging out and wanted to buy some beer to help them pass the hot summer day away. Charles had a laid-back demeanor and was always befriending strangers, especially the females. When they were purchasing the beer inside the Handy Andy, Charles befriended one of the stock boys. This stock boy told Charles and Benny that if they would hang out in the store parking lot, he would bring them out some free beer. Charles and Benny were glad to take him up on his offer.

The stock boy had also told the same thing to some of

his friends. The friends had all joined Charles and Benny in this impromptu beer party. They opened the doors to Charles' car and turned up the rock and roll. They were there for about three hours and all the while the stock boy had kept bringing them some ice-cold beer for the boys to drink.

At 8:00 P.M. the stock boy had told them that he was getting off duty and that he would join in on the party. He arrived with more beer and everyone cheered and gave high fives all around. After the stock boy drank six beers, he began to get unruly and began trying to pick a fight with Charles. He obviously could not handle his liquor and Charles was not the right person to pick a fight with either. Charles was a big, rough and tough guy. He had a reputation for being one of the best fighters in town. Charles was like Jephthah of the bible, a mean and tough misfit, and natural born fighter. Pancho knew that he could trust Charles with his life.

Charles tried to ignore the stock boy, but he kept on insisting and telling Charles, "You think you're so bad, don't you, just because you're a big dude? I bet I can whip you."

Charles had even tried reverse psychology, "Yep, I bet you can whip me. Let's just forget about it and drink some more beer."

The stock boy kept on pestering Charles and finally Charles told him, "Look, if you want to fight, I'll fight you, but I really don't want to fight you."

The stock boy threw a beer bottle at Charles and hit him on the back as Charles turned and ducked to avoid a direct blow to the face. Charles told him, "Well if you're looking for trouble, I'm the man to see."

Charles had put his beer down on the parking lot and walked toward the stock boy like John Wayne on a mission full of confidence and malevolence. When Charles reached the stock boy he swung with a hard, straight right hand to his face followed immediately by a left and another right to the face. He then grabbed the stock boy by the neck with his left hand and held him at arms length. The stock boy was caught off guard and did not expect Charles to be so efficient with his punches. He tried throwing punches but could not reach Charles, so he decided to kick him in the groin and the legs. This only irritated Charles even more. Charles said, "So you really want to fight. Okay, here we go!"

Charles picked up the stock boy with both hands and lifted him up above his head and body slammed him directly onto his face on the pavement. Blood and teeth splattered all over Charles' steel-toed biker boots. The stock boy's friends did not even flinch, they were not about to get involved and end up in the same predicament. Benny Low didn't say a word either. He had seen Charles in action before and he knew that his help was not needed unless some one jumped in for the stock boy, and besides, Benny was a lover not a fighter.

Charles picked up the stock boy by the neck and hit him with three hard rights to the face. He then lifted the stock boy again and body slammed him once more onto his face on the pavement. The stock boy was out cold for five minutes. When he woke up, he was in extreme pain due to his teeth being knocked out, his mouth and nose ruptured, and his eyes swollen from the blows to the face. He rose to his feet and had begun to cry out loud and shout at Charles, "I'm going to get you dude! Nobody does this to me. I'm going to go and get a gun and take care of you." He then limped away and went out of sight.

Charles told Benny that he was going to go home because he didn't want any more trouble. Benny tried to discourage him from leaving, "There's still a whole lot of beer. Why don't you stay and drink some more?"

Charles answered, "I better go. If this dude comes back, I don't want to hurt him anymore."

Charles got into his car and left the scene. Benny stayed behind with the friends of the stock boy and they continued with their merry celebration.

The stock boy had arrived at the Handy Andy parking lot looking for Charles with a .38 special in his hand and revenge boiling in his heart. Everyone told him that Charles had already left and would not be coming back. The stock boy was so enraged at not finding Charles that he stood still for a few seconds, then let out a horrendous scream at the top of his lungs to express his anger and frustration. He was so angry that his entire body was shaking, and tears were streaming down his tattered face.

He wanted Charles to pay for the damage he had done to him not only physically, but mentally and emotionally as well. Everyone was uneasy due to the stock boy brandishing a handgun, but they never expected what happened next. As the stock boy stood still and quivering with rage, he contemplated his next move. He thought that if he couldn't kill Charles, he would strike at the next best thing afforded to him at the moment.

That would be Charles' buddy Benny Low. In an instant the stock boy made a decision that would haunt him for the rest of his life. He spun around and made his way toward

Benny who was very drunk and very unsuspecting. The stock boy stood directly in front of Benny and said, "You're going to pay for this!"

He aimed the gun squarely at Benny's forehead and pulled the trigger. Benny fell to the ground and lay there in a massive puddle of blood barely hanging on to life by a thin sliver of thread.

Benny had ended up in the intensive care unit at the Bexar County hospital where he remained for six months. The forefront of his skull had been shattered and his brain injured by the perilous bullet. He always had a slight stutter, but now it would really be pronounced. The doctors, however, gave Benny a good prognosis saying that there was no permanent brain damage and that his skull would eventually heal up.

The stock boy was arrested for attempted murder and sentenced to three years in a state penitentiary. It had been reported to Pancho that life was hard for the stock boy in prison. The last account Pancho heard was that they had turned the stock boy into a girl.

When Benny was released from the hospital, he went to visit a girlfriend of his on the West Side of town. Benny was a very handsome young man with a thin physique, light skin, long wavy brown hair, and hazel eyes. Many people had thought that he looked like the man on the Zig-Zag rolling papers cover. He had been a track star in Jr. High and High School which made him very popular throughout the city. He had many girlfriends at his beck and call. He had girls to the left of him and girls to the right.

This girl that he had gone to visit, however, was his favorite. Her name was Dollar Forty-Nine. She had earned this nickname during her elementary school days. A classmate had told her that he would give her $1.49 for a kiss and a hickey on his neck. She was more than willing to oblige with great fervor and delight. Word had gotten around school of her low-priced deed and the name stuck with her. Everyone called her this throughout her Jr. High and High School days. Many people didn't know the story of how she had gotten the name, but nonetheless this was what they called her.

To say that Dollar Forty-Nine was beautiful was a gross understatement. She had grown up to be a real knock out. She was supermodel beautiful. She was slender with fair silky skin, and straight light brown hair that went down to her waist. The thing that really stood out on Dollar Forty-Nine was her violet colored eyes. This was a rare physical trait, but the fact that a *Chicana* from San Antonio had violet colored eyes made Dollar Forty-Nine really extraordinary.

Where did she get her violet eyes? Rumor had it that Dollar Forty-Nine's mother had an affair with a German musician that played in a very popular *Conjunto* band. Pancho had read that Elizabeth Taylor had violet colored eyes, but he did not believe that any human being could have such a physical trait. Not until he met Dollar Forty-Nine in person when she had shown up with Benny Low at his brother Pistol Pete's party. Even though Benny Low had many girlfriends, he was recently thinking of setting himself apart for Dollar Forty-Nine.

Benny's parents had tried to dissuade him from going out to the West Side of town. Benny still had his entire head in bandages and was still recovering from the wounds. But Benny wanted to see Dollar Forty-Nine and let her know of his plan to exclusively get together with her. So he went in spite of his parent's objections.

He and Dollar Forty-Nine were talking about their relationship and catching up on current events as they stood on her front lawn. All the while Benny kept trying to steal a kiss or two throughout the evening. At 10:00 P.M. Benny was about to say good bye to Dollar Forty-Nine and go back home. He was feeling tired and wanted to get some rest. Unexpectedly, a group of young thugs belonging to a local west side gang called "*Los* Really Rottens *de la calle Chupaderas*" had walked by. The leader of the gang, Andy the Bird, was a rather small man in stature, but was cold-blooded and down right mean. He was called the bird because his nose looked like the beak on a bird.

As the Really Rottens walked passed Dollar Forty-Nine's house, Andy the Bird noticed that Benny was a stranger and was not from their neighborhood. Coming to the Rottens' home turf without their permission was the worst thing a stranger could have done.

Andy the Bird walked up to Benny and said, "Who are you and why are you in my neighborhood without my permission?"

Dollar Forty-Nine quickly chimed in and told Andy the Bird, "He's with me so you better back off or I'll call the police on you."

She realized that Andy the Bird meant business, so she ran inside to call the police. Benny told Andy the Bird, "I don't want any trouble. I'm just here pledging my love to Dollar Forty-Nine."

Andy the Bird said, "I'll pledge something to you" as he leaned forward and punched Benny on the head.

Benny felt a sharp pain and ringing rush through his head as his almost healed wounds were opened up again. Before Benny was able to defend himself or run (remember, he was a track star), two of the Really Rottens had grabbed him by the arms so Andy the Bird could continue his assault. Much to everyone's surprise Andy the Bird took out an eight-inch switch blade from his back pocket and stabbed Benny on the chest and stomach seven times.

The Really Rottens immediately ran and fled the scene. Dollar Forty-Nine came outside and found Benny slumped over on the ground. It took the ambulance twenty minutes before they showed up and rendered aid to Benny. He had lost a lot of blood, his left lung was punctured, and his spleen had been damaged, but he was still alive. He had spent another three months in the hospital and pulled through with another miraculous recovery.

When Benny was released from the hospital he wanted to speak with Dollar Forty-Nine, but he was not about to go visit her again. He had had enough of hospitals, surgeries, and bed pans. Benny had a twelve-inch scar running up his chest due to the exploratory surgery the doctors performed to try and figure out what was the extent of the knife wounds. He had lengthy bandages wrapped around his chest which his mother had to help him change and clean his wounds each night before he went to bed.

Benny's home telephone had been disconnected due to the financial strain the hospital bills were causing. Benny decided to walk to the corner of his street, which was less than fifty feet away from his house, and use the public telephone. Everyone in the neighborhood knew Benny and liked him and his family so this seemed like a harmless proposal. The public telephone was set up in a blue-colored aluminum non-enclosed phone booth with no covering to help keep the elements away from the user.

Benny slowly hobbled his way to the phone booth and called Dollar Forty-Nine. They said some polite greetings and whispered their sweet nothings and then continued the conversation they were having before Benny was stabbed. They must have been talking on the phone for approximately thirty minutes when Benny heard a loud roaring sound approaching him.

The phone booth was exactly on the corner of St. Mary's street and Lotus Avenue in front of the Church's Fried Chicken restaurant. To Benny's left was the St. Mary's street infamous underpass. The underpass had been built in order to allow the Southern Pacific Railways to pass through the city without hindering or stopping traffic flow. The underpass was in between Roosevelt Park and Brackenridge High School. On one occasion, when Pancho was eight years old, a train had derailed and fell unto the underpass and landed on top of a vehicle which was carrying a man and his young daughter. Pancho had heard what sounded like a great explosion while playing outside of his house. He and Andrew walked over to the underpass and saw the vehicle that was completely smashed to one foot in height.

Benny had looked up to see if he could ascertain what the loud sound was and noticed that it was a candy apple red, two door, 1969 Chevy Camaro coming up the underpass at full speed. The driver of the car was a young seventeen-year-old named Robert V. He had three adolescent female passengers that he had recently picked up on SW Military Drive. Robert V. was trying to impress the girls with his shiny red car and its capability to accelerate to very high speeds.

They had made their way down Roosevelt Street passing red lights and racing past any vehicle on the road. They were on their way to cruise the streets of downtown San Antonio. When Robert V. approached the underpass, he had been traveling at seventy miles per hour. The car was well built and was handling the high rate of speed and all the curves in the road very well. When they were coming out of the underpass the street curved to the left, but Robert V. was distracted at the moment. He had been looking at the female front passenger who was wearing some very revealing short-shorts.

Robert V. had looked up and noticed the curve in the road. He slightly turned the steering wheel to the left, but it was too much to the left. He quickly jerked the wheel to the right, but had over-corrected. This had caused the car to swerve wildly to the left then to the right. Robert V. lost control of the car and due to the high rate of speed it flipped over on its side and rolled over continuously for fifty feet then crushed the phone booth with Benny in it.

The three young girls had died at the scene. One girl died from a head injury. Another girl died from internal bleeding. The other girl's neck had been broken in the impact. None of them had been wearing their seat belts. The driver had his left arm sticking outside of the window and it was completely torn away from his body in the roll over, but he did not die.

Benny had been hit so hard that his white, high top Converse All Stars were blown off of his feet. Benny had been steam rolled and thrown some fifty feet from the corner. Both of his arms had been broken, and both of his legs had been broken along with five ribs. He also sustained another major head injury. No one expected him to be alive after this collision, but he was.

Benny had pulled through yet another calamity to live and tell about it. The unluckiest man in San Antonio had been knocked down again, but not knocked out of the game of life. Pancho had asked Benny, "Why do you think all of this has happened to you and you're still here to talk about it?"

Benny answered, "God has spared me and set me apart for something. What it is, I don't know. All I know is that I'm here, I'm alive, and I'm ready for whatever God wants me to do. It's good to be alive!"

CHAPTER 10

WAKE UP THE DEAD

As far back as Pancho could remember, his entire family, including aunts, uncles, third cousins, grandparents, and anybody associated with his family had severely abused alcohol. He thought that this was a normal way of life. He really believed that every family in America experienced this phenomenon. He and his four brothers followed the same pattern.

His earliest recollections were those of his parents drinking with family and friends and then having a knock down, drag out fight in the streets. He remembered waking up on Saturday mornings and turning the TV on to Bugs Bunny cartoons. He would frequently see his father passed out cold underneath the kitchen table and his mother passed out cold on the bathroom floor. This was very typical for the Martinez household.

By the time Pancho was seventeen, he had become an alcoholic and needed to drink alcohol every day of the week. If he didn't have the money for the alcohol he would steal to support his dreadful habit.

Pancho's mother was weary of her entire family being alcoholics, the life they were leading, and seeing her life and that of her children going from bad to worse each day. She wanted a way out of the misery brought on by the drug of their choice. She could no longer fight and felt totally alone. This was not the first-time problems had come into her life. She had struggled with sickness, marital problems, family problems, persistent depression, and had hoped that they would all go away by drowning in a bottle. But they didn't. They only got worse. Deep within herself she felt sick and miserable. She had sought out help from her friends, husband, and children, but no one could help. So she turned to the professionals.

She went to a psychologist and explained her perilous predicament of a life so stressful and painful that at times it dropped her to her knees. But the psychologist told her, "I'm sorry lady, but there is no hope for you and your family. You see, there is no cure for alcoholism, so you and your family are doomed to die in this miserable and wretched circumstance."

She left his office in tears, feeling heartbroken and hopeless. She loved her family and did not want them to suffer this terrible fate, so she set up an appointment with a psychiatrist.

She explained her story to the psychiatrist and he told her, "I'm sorry lady, but alcoholism is hereditary so there is no hope for you and your family. You see, there is no cure for alcoholism, so you and your family are doomed to die in this miserable and wretched circumstance."

Again, she broke down in tears and wept bitterly for herself and her family. She thought to herself, "There has to be someone that can help me and my family. There just has to be."

She pondered the thought for a long while and then it dawned on her to go speak with a Roman Catholic Priest. If anyone could help her, she contemplated, it would be the Catholic Church.

When she met with the priest she tried to explain her situation, but he seemed disinterested and cut her off and asked her candidly, "Are you married through the Roman Catholic Church?"

Pancho's mother was stunned by his question. Didn't he want to know about their struggle with alcohol? After all, this was the reason that she came to speak with him about. But the priest insisted with a spiteful voice, "Are you married through the church?"

"No," was her reply as she hung her head in shame. "Then I can not help you! You and your family are doomed to die in this miserable and wretched circumstance," was the priest's terse reply.

She walked out of there thinking, "If the church can't help me, then I'm really in trouble. Not even God can forgive me for what I'm doing and the example I'm setting for my family." She had come to the end of her line.

She had contemplated suicide and thought of taking some valium that the psychiatrist prescribed to her when she tried to get his help. She thought it would be best for her to take her own life because she could no longer live like this watching her children suffer in alcohol. She had gathered the pills and tried to swallow them on two separate occasions. Each time her brash attempts were thwarted by someone or something waking her up from her drunken stupor with the pills still in her hand and some scattered about the floor where she was sprawled in an awkward twisted position.

After her second attempt she found herself alone, sitting on the floor of her bedroom with no doctors, no miracle medicine, and no strength left to continue. She just sat there feeling dull, miserable, aching, and with no hope. It was while she was there that a strange fear came upon her; a fear that she had never felt before. She lifted herself off of the floor and sat on the bed and looked toward a corner of the room where she had a picture of Jesus. She had begun to cry uncontrollably but didn't even know why she was crying so much. She called out to Jesus himself, "If you are really there Jesus, help me because I cannot find any help here and I don't know what to do!"

A few days later she had begun to scroll through the yellow pages looking for telephone numbers of local churches to see if someone could help her. She didn't know what she was looking for, all she knew was that something kept telling her to keep looking through the phone book and call a church. She called several churches, and some did answer and would ask her, "What do you want? What is it you are looking for?"

She would respond, "I don't know what I want, and I don't know what I'm looking for. I don't even know why I called you."

One pastor that had answered the phone told her, "Lady, you are searching for God. Don't let anyone or anything take that out of your head. Keep searching for God and read your bible." He had invited her to his church, but she could not muster up the courage to go.

She kept scrolling through the phone book and calling

church after church. Finally, a pastor told her he would go to her house and speak to her if she would like. She said yes. Pancho was there when the Pastor arrived and remembers seeing a lofty, lean, Anglo American cowboy come into their house and speak with his mother. That day, on their living room floor, Pancho's mother knelt down and asked Jesus to forgive her of all of her sins and invited him to be her personal savior.

She was never the same after that day. She stopped drinking alcohol, using profanity, and began to attend the pastor's church regularly. All she wanted to do now was to go to church and read her bible. Pancho thought that his mother was experiencing a phase that all women go through when they reach a certain age. The phase would soon pass, and she would be back to her normal self with the drinking, profanity and fighting. Or so he thought.

Pancho's mother had never learned to drive so she would ask her husband for a ride to church. But her husband would refuse to take her. She had a new desire within her soul and spirit and this desire was motivating her to go to church, so she persisted. On one Sunday, she had gotten dressed and sat down in the living room waiting for her husband to take her to church. He entered the living room and asked her, "What are you doing sitting in the living room all dressed up?"

She answered, "I want to go to church and I'm expecting you to take me to church."

Her husband was furious at her demand and exclaimed, "I will not take you to church, and that is final."

Pancho's mother had begun to cry with her head in her hands. Pancho's father did not know how to respond to the situation. He was used to his wife fighting and cussing him out if he refused to do something she wanted to do. "I only want to go to church," she whispered softly.

Pancho's father felt embarrassed and ashamed at his stubbornness so he gave in and dropped her off at church. He took her a second time and then a third. After the third time he had taken her to church he confronted her and said, "You have something going on at that church. You obviously are seeing another man there."

He was sure that his wife was having an affair with someone in the church. That would explain why she always wanted to be at church. On the following Friday, Pancho's father decided to sneak into the church after he dropped off his wife for a Friday night service meeting to find out whom she was allegedly seeing. He had been drinking alcohol and entered the church through a back door holding a huge knife in his hand.

He sat in the rear of the sanctuary and waited for his wife to sit down. He thought to himself, "Whichever man she sits next to will be the one she is involved with in the affair. I will confront the man and stab him to death in front of everyone in the church."

Pancho's mother did not sit next to anyone. Pancho's mother sat alone. By this time the service had already begun. The lights had been dimmed and the praise and worship music had begun to be played. Pancho's father had decided to stay and keep an eye on his wife.

By the end of the service Pancho's father had sobered up and had paid attention to the pastor's sermon. When the invitation was given Pancho's father went forward and accepted Jesus Christ as his personal savior.

Now Pancho's father had stopped drinking as well. All

he wanted to do was go to church with his wife. Pancho had thought that this was just too weird. He thought that his mother's unusual behavior was due to a phase that women go through. His father's behavior, however, was unexplainable. This was a man who had been involved with alcohol almost his entire life and never really wanted to go to church. Pancho's father was a man who had seen the devil himself.

Pancho's father would tell a story about working in Geronimo, Texas picking fruit when he was a young man. He and two friends of his had gone to work clearing the fields of weeds. They would spend the night in their dilapidated van. There were many other people there as well. Some of the women that lived in the main house of the ranch would prepare meals for them.

There was an old man, the caretaker of the ranch, who would stay up at night and tell the young men ghost stories. One night after the ghost stories, he asked them if they believed in the devil. They all laughed and sarcastically said, "No, of course we don't believe in the devil."

The old man had begun to get angry and told the young men that the devil did exist. The old man stood up and went behind a huge barn. Next, he built a huge bonfire. He then had begun to call out to Lucifer. Pancho's father said this was the first time he had ever heard anyone use that name for the devil. The old man continued to call out to the devil all night. The young men laughed at him and went to bed.

In the middle of the night they were awakened by a huge windstorm. The entire van was shaking violently. They looked out of the windshield of the van and noticed something big and black in front of the van. It repeatedly kept going forward toward the van and then backward away from the van. At first, they had thought it was a big piece of tumble weed. They turned on the headlights to the van. They saw an oversized, black, wild turkey with its wings outstretched. The mammoth turkey had begun to gobble, gurgle and shriek loudly and rapidly. The rabid turkey had then proceeded to attack the van. This scared the young men to death. They turned off the headlights, crawled under their covers and prayed themselves to sleep.

In the morning they asked the women and others in the house if they had been awakened by the windstorm. No one had even known that there was a windstorm. Some that had been awake throughout the night said that there was no storm and that it had been a quiet peaceful night.

⚜ CHAPTER 11 ⚜

ARE YOU READY FOR A MIRACLE?

As Pancho Martinez opened his eyes, he felt a sense of peace come over his mind and entire body. He didn't know where this peace came from or why it was there. He looked up and saw Stella's angry husband still standing there cursing, fretting, and spitting like a rabid dog in heat. This man meant business and apparently this would be Pancho Martinez's last stand. This would be Pancho's Little Big Horn.

Pancho had gone too far this time. He thought of Jethro Tull's song "Up to Me." He thought to himself, "I've gone too far. I've been left at a wimpy bar. I made the scene at Cousin Jack's but I can't put the bottles back to mend the glasses that I cracked."

Pancho knew that he had finally gone over the edge and worshipped the golden calf. He had become the all-time loser and now he was going head-long straight to his death. He looked over at Stella and had noticed that she was crying profoundly and pleading with her husband not to pull the trigger. Pancho felt sympathy and compassion for Stella in her present predicament. She had been through so much hardship and now this was going to be one more wretched event to add to her solemn life. Pancho wanted to hold Stella close to him and console her by running his hands through her hair, but the moment had not lent itself to his thoughtful offer.

Instead he whispered a prayer. In all sincerity he declared; "Jesus, you are the God of everything, please let me lean upon you gently. I'm calling on you to save me. I stand before you in my ugly presence. Jesus, save me!"

Pancho looked around the room and continued with his whispered prayer. "The Hollywood hero is in need. I need the God high in heaven to smile down upon me. I am not using your name in vain. Jesus save me, I don't want to die."

As Pancho prayed and deliberated, the angry husband yelled at Stella, "You are mine Stella! You are my wife! The dish will not run away with the spoon today. I will not let anyone take you away from me! I love you!"

His voice had turned to a whimper as he continued to tell Stella, "I love you! I love you!"

The angry husband was half-way turned facing toward Stella. Pancho saw a chance to pounce on the man and take his weapon away from him. Just as Pancho was about to leap into the air and grab the man's gun, the angry husband turned toward Pancho with his eyes glazed over appearing crazy and deranged. The angry husband pulled the trigger, and emptied the gun firing all six bullets.

The gun shots were so loud that Pancho's ears immediately began to ring thunderously. Pancho told himself, "I'm dead. Within the next millisecond I will feel a sharp pain in my chest and it won't slow down. The searing hot bullets will penetrate my body and then I will drop to the ground dead as a door nail."

One second went by. Stella shouted in fright and fell to the ground in deep despair and continued to sob uncontrollably because the love of her life, Pancho Martinez, had been shot dead. Two seconds went by. The angry, jealous husband wasn't so angry anymore. He was scared now; scared at having just shot a man in cold blood. He unsteadily dropped the smoking, empty gun to the ground with remorse and dread. Three seconds went by. There was no sharp pain in Pancho's chest, and Pancho had not fallen to the ground. How could this be?

All six bullets had missed Pancho. How could anyone have missed such a shot from six feet away? Even a blind man could have hit a target from that distance.

At that very moment God had decided to intervene in the situation. God made the bullets travel sideways and away from Pancho Martinez. God heard Pancho's plea for help and answered. It was a classic, full-fledged, stinking miracle of divine intervention.

Pancho had heard about God and his miracles and his book of rules since he was a young boy. He had always believed that God did indeed exist. He had just witnessed God's miraculous power with his own eyes. Pancho had been rescued before, but never in this manner; never directly from the hand of God. As Pancho contemplated what had just occurred, his mind wandered to the time when God had indirectly intervened in his life in just the nick of time.

One warm Saturday afternoon on the tenth day of March, Pancho, Jabber Jaw, Disco Henry, Andrew, and

Psycho Michael were hanging out at Roosevelt Park. They had been wasting the day away by ogling some teenage girls that were enjoying a birthday party with their families. Pancho's cousin Mando was driving by in his brand new 1979 Cadillac Eldorado and stopped by to say hello.

The Cadillac had obviously been purchased with illegal funds since Mando was only a junior in high school. The car had been paid in full with hard, cold cash. Mando had asked the boys if they wanted to go for a drive and smoke some Columbian Gold marijuana. Of course, the boys had immediately jumped in for the ride.

The performance, smooth suspension, luxury, and comfort of the new Cadillac were superb. The premium Bose six speaker surround sound system was blaring with ZZ Top's "I'm Bad, I'm Nationwide." As the rowdy group rolled South down Roosevelt Street they were all singing in unison, "Easing down the highway in a new Cadillac, I had a fine fox in front, I had primo in the back."

The song did not say that "primo" was in the back, but since Pancho was Mando's cousin, the boys had decided to change the lyrics to fit the moment. When they reached SW Military Drive, Mando decided to pull into Harlandale Park to chill out for awhile. The boys poured out of the car and stood in a circle under the shade of some willow trees. They were filled with excitement and gratification of being alive and enjoying life to its fullest according to their Southside standards.

They all cheered, gave high-fives, patted each other on the back and said, "It doesn't get any better than this. It's a beautiful day and it's good to be alive. We are riding in a brand new Cadillac listening to some cool rock and roll, smoking some great weed, and hanging out with our best friends."

Disco Henry spoke up and said, "You all are my best friends. I would do anything for you guys. I would even die for you."

He then pulled out a stainless-steel ball point hammer that he had concealed in the back of his pants. The hammer was unusual in that it had a big ball on one end of the head and a sharp point on the other. Henry shouted, "If anyone messes with us I will do some damage," as he swung the hammer in the air mimicking an attack on someone.

Jabber Jaw Anthony pulled out a ten-inch Bowie knife and repeated what Henry had just said. Psycho Michael, Andrew, Mando and Pancho had all concurred and lifted up their right hands straight up in the air and yelled like the American Indians did before they went into battle.

Mando told the boys, "I'm down to my last joint so you better savor the moment."

The boys suddenly noticed a two-door, 1969 Chevy Camaro with gray primer coming into the park. It pulled up and parked beside them with four, much older, Hispanic males onboard. The four guys had gotten out of the Camaro and started to walk calmly toward the boys. The driver was approximately six feet tall with long brown hair, had an athletic build, was very good looking, and was wearing some tight fitting faded blue jeans. The front passenger was approximately five-feet-seven with a thick goatee and was wearing a "wife beater" under shirt with brown khaki shorts that went down to his calves. He was drinking whiskey from a thirty-two ounce glass pickle jar. He obviously was some kind of *Cholo* Westsider. The other two guys had stayed in the background and were trying to be inconspicuous.

As they continued to approach, Mando whispered to Pancho, "I know the driver from McCollum High School."

The driver had walked up to Mando, who was standing beside Pancho, and said, "What's up man? Do you have any weed?"

Pancho had assumed that they were Mando's friends or acquaintances, so he didn't give them much thought. Besides, his mind was peacefully drifting due to the Columbian Gold and Riot's "Swords and Tequila" song that was currently playing on the Caddy's radio. Pancho squatted down in order to listen to the song without being interrupted.

The driver continued questioning Mando, "Do you have any weed? I want you to give me some weed."

Mando answered him, "I don't have anymore weed. All I have is this joint that we're smoking right now. You and your buddies are welcome to join us and take some hits off of it."

The driver replied, "Look, I want you to give me some weed and I want you to give it to me right now."

This had caught Pancho's attention and made him think that the driver was out of line and looking for trouble. Just then, and unexpectedly, the driver took a swing at Mando with his right elbow. Mando saw it coming and moved back in order to avoid the blow intended for his face. Mando quickly threw a right of his own and hit the driver squarely on the face. Pancho was stunned that these guys had the guts to confront him and his friends. Didn't they know that Henry was packing a hammer, and Anthony his Bowie knife? Didn't they know that they had just pledged their lives for one another?

As Pancho was in deep thought, the Cholo passenger spilled the whiskey onto the ground and stuck his fist inside of the pickle jar and hit Pancho on top of his head with it. The pickle jar did not break, but Pancho could feel the pain on his skull begin to engulf him. Pancho immediately stood up and looked the Cholo in the eyes and quoted Dirty Harry, "You've got to ask yourself one question: 'Do I feel lucky?' Well, do ya, punk?"

He then proceeded to throw four and five punch combinations to the Cholo's face. The Cholo was caught off guard by Pancho's assault and fell to the ground semi-conscious. Pancho turned around and saw Mando and the driver rolling around on the ground in a struggle. He quickly ran over to help his cousin and grabbed the driver by his long brown hair and kicked him twice directly on the face with his steel toed biker boots. The driver yelled hysterically and released Mando.

Pancho and Mando stood side by side and had begun to laugh. Mando said, "I'm sure glad you're on my side. Remember when we were little, and our parents made us fight against each other?"

Pancho recalled the time when he was six years old and he and his friends would play like they were other people. They did this to say who was tougher or who could beat up the other. One kid would say, "I'm Muhammad Ali."

The other would say, "I'm George Foreman."

One would say, "I'm Chuck Norris, no one can beat me up."

Then the other kid would say, "I'm Bruce Lee. I can beat

up anybody." They would go around and around picking names of different people until Pancho would finally say, "I'm Samson. I'm in the bible so no one can beat me up because God is on my side and no one can beat up God."

His friends would be upset, but they would all concede and agree with him that no one could beat up God.

On one particular occasion Pancho's family had been drinking in their front yard on a Friday night and making the kids box each other. Pancho's dad told him to box his cousin Mando (who was two years older) because he was beating up everybody. Pancho's dad said, "I bet he can't beat Pancho."

Pancho told his cousin Mando that he was Muhammad Ali and Mando said that he was George Foreman. They went around and around until Pancho finally said that he was Samson. Mando then proceeded to beat Pancho to a pulp. Pancho took off the gloves and tried to strangle and bite Mando saying, "You're not supposed to beat up Samson."

The handsome driver stood up with his face completely bloodied and stared at Mando and Pancho with unbelief. Then he proceeded to say, "You will pay for this! I'm going to get my gun and kill all of you!"

He then went to his car and opened the trunk to get his gun. Andrew immediately told his buddies that he was still recovering from the gun shot wound to his calf, so he was not about to stick around and face another shooter's onslaught. Andrew had started to hurriedly hop away. Henry threw his hammer to the ground and said, "I'm not going up against a gun. I'm out of here."

Henry joined Andrew and ran away from the scene.

Psycho and Jabber Jaw hastily followed Henry in order to escape the attack that was about to ensue. Mando and Pancho stood by themselves wondering what the driver's next move would be. Pancho thought to himself as he saw his friends running away, "What happened to 'I'll die for you?' What happened to 'If anybody messes with us I'll do some damage?' What happened to all that?"

The driver was slumped over moving items around in the trunk and then appeared with a long object in his hands. At first, Pancho thought that it was a rifle. Then Pancho looked again and realized that it was a double-edged axe with a thirty-six-inch wooden handle. Pancho was relieved that it wasn't a gun, but became traumatized at the thought of being cut in half with the axe and seeing the lower half of his body left discarded and bleeding on the ground. He had never been attacked by anyone yielding an axe. Some people he had fought against had pulled out knives, guns, bottles, sticks, and rocks, but never an axe.

Pancho was contemplating his defense against the driver and his axe when the driver lunged at them with a wild banshee yell and began swinging the axe at Mando and Pancho. Mando moved left and Pancho went right. The driver chased after Mando. Pancho made a full circle to see how he could help out his cousin.

Even though he was scared to death of the axe, he was not about to run like his friends for he had meant what he had said earlier. Besides, Mando was blood so he had to stay and fight. If he ran, how could he ever face his father and mother or his aunt and uncle and say that he left Mando alone to fend for himself. It was part of the Chicano heritage, it had been written in their DNA – you never run and leave a blood relative alone when in a fight.

Mando was running away from the driver who was in hot pursuit and swinging the axe. Mando stopped and picked up a huge decaying log and swung it at the driver and hit him directly on his bloodied face. The driver fell to the ground. This gave Mando enough time to run back toward Pancho so they could make their getaway from this madman intent on killing them both.

As Mando approached, Pancho said, "Let's get out of here! We can't fight against an axe!"

They both had begun to run leaving Mando's new, shiny Cadillac behind. Mando said, "I've got to get my car. What will I tell my dad?"

Pancho answered, "We'll get it, but we'll have to come back once these guys leave."

They looked ahead of them and noticed Andrew, Henry, Jabber Jaw, and Psycho standing and talking with several men. As they drew closer Pancho noticed that he recognized some of these guys. It was Robert and Richard Ramirez and some of their family members.

Robert and Richard Ramirez were at the park celebrating a birthday for one of their family members along with a bunch of their aunts, uncles, cousins, nieces and nephews. Richard, who was a Golden Gloves champ, told Pancho that Andrew and Psycho had explained to them the situation with the driver and his three buddies. Richard came up to Pancho and shook his hand and said, "Me and my family are going to back you up. You are a good friend. You are one of us and if anybody messes with one of us, they have to mess with all of us."

One of Richard's uncles, who must have been in his early thirties, picked up a thin stick about twenty-four inches long and led the procession back toward the vehicle of the four hoodlums that had ruined their beautiful and tranquil afternoon.

Pancho could see that the four hoodlums had jumped into their car and were attempting to make a getaway from the huge crowd of about twenty that was approaching them. But their Camaro wouldn't start. If ever there was a bad time for a vehicle to stall, it was then. The four guys stepped out of the vehicle and stood in front of it awaiting Pancho and the others to arrive as if to indicate that they were going to take a stand and fight.

The driver stood with the axe hoisted upon his shoulder and ready to strike. Richard's skinny uncle walked directly up to the driver defiantly without fear of the axe or trepidation of any kind and began to poke at his chest with the thin stick and inquired of his intentions. The driver did not know how to respond. He told Richard's uncle, "We just want to get out of here. We don't want any trouble."

Richard's uncle answered, "It's too late. You came looking for trouble and now you found it!"

Richard's uncle threw the small stick at the driver's face and punched him in the eye three times causing the driver to lose control of the axe and drop it to the ground.

The other three hoodlums began to run like someone had fired the starting gun to a race. Robert Ramirez had picked up Henry's hammer along the way and chased one of the two inconspicuous hoodlums and hit him on the side of the head with the pointed end of the hammer. Needless to say, the hoodlum fell to the ground in a thud. Robert continued to hit him on the face and head several more times with the hammer.

The other inconspicuous hoodlum was being kicked and punched as he lay huddled on the ground. The Cholo was surrounded by five people with one holding him up so the others could hit him on his face. The driver was being dragged by his hair as six others were kicking and punching him all over his body. Pancho and Mando and their four buddies stood and watched in amazement as the Ramirez family swarmed the four hoodlums in their defense.

Pancho was grateful that God had elected to directly intervene in his life and rescue him from certain death by Stella's fourth husband's .44 Magnum assault. The three figures had stood motionless in the room, stunned and very much surprised. Stella was relieved that Pancho was unharmed. The only person on the scene that wasn't glad to see that Pancho was still alive was Stella's weeping husband. "I know that he's going to kill me now," he thought to himself.

Stella had thought the same thing. So, she slowly and quietly moved toward her husband in order to protect him from the certain death that was impending. She did not understand why she was protecting a man that she detested. Maybe she was trying to protect Pancho from committing a terrible crime. She locked her arms around the man that she could barely stand. Stella smiled lovingly at Pancho and fluttered her eyelashes and broke the deep silence in the cold drafty room and said, "I thought that your luck had finally run out Pancho."

There was a long awkward pause as she waited in vain for Pancho to respond. She searched deep within her heart for her next words. "I'll miss you," she said to Pancho.

Stella knew that this would be the end of her relationship with Pancho. She was standing next to her abhorrent husband, but her heart was leaning toward Pancho Martinez.

Pancho knew that Stella was trying to protect this loathsome man. Stella's husband just stood there clutching her waist and staring into space not knowing what Pancho's next move would be. Pancho began to move toward the pair now huddled near the corner with a regal and defiant sway in his steps. He stood directly in front of Stella and took a long, hard look at her face. He noticed her fair skin and tender, amorous eyes. He leaned over and whispered in her ear with a grin, "Goodbye my rare and radiant maiden whom the angels name Lenore. Quoth the Raven – 'Nevermore.'"

This, of course, was a quote from Edgar Allen Poe's *The Raven*. Pancho was telling Stella that their relationship was over. He was telling Stella that he would never see her again. Then he walked away with his face held down and made his usual exit through the back door.

❧ CHAPTER 12 ❧

DO YOU SMELL LIKE GOD?

Pancho went directly to his parent's home and told them the events of that evening. His parents told him that God and his angels were watching over him and that he needed to go to church with them to find out more about this God that had just spared him his life. Pancho wanted to find out more about God, but he didn't want to go to, what he thought was, his parent's "Born Again," boring Baptist church. His parents attended Theo Avenue Baptist Church in the South Side of San Antonio.

Pancho had been brought up by his parents as a Roman Catholic. Pancho was a C.I.N.O. (pronounced Chēno; using the Latin pronunciation of the letter c) – Catholic In Name Only. He called himself a Roman Catholic, but he rarely went to church and did not practice any of the teachings of the church. He would go to church involuntarily on Christmas or Easter because his mother would twist his ears and say, "You're going to go to church whether you want to or not."

Pancho would attend the Christmas midnight masses

after drinking a few beers and getting high on some marijuana. He would try to follow along and stand up and sit down at the appropriate times, but he was never able to get the ritual down just right. He would look at the elderly lady's sitting around him and follow them. If they stood up, he'd get up. If they sat down, he'd sit down.

Pancho had tried to go about his life as usual and tried to forget about God and how he miraculously saved his life on that fateful day, but he couldn't. God kept on trying to woo Pancho and get his attention fixed on him. Pancho would go to see a movie and the plot revolved around trust in God. He would hear a new Rock song on the radio and it mentioned God's name. Everywhere he turned, God was there patiently waiting for Pancho.

Pancho's parents would routinely invite him to go to church with them, but he was obstinate in his own beliefs in the Roman Catholic Church. His mother challenged him one day and said, "If you don't want to go to church, then at least read the bible. I challenge you to read the bible."

Pancho took her up on it. He was going to read the entire bible. He would use all of his knowledge and education to prove to his mom that the Roman Catholic religion was superior to the Baptist religion.

Pancho had begun to read the bible from Genesis 1:1. Every night before he went to bed he would read a small portion of the bible. The stories were enthralling, but he saw them as interesting fairy tales. That is, until he arrived at Exodus 19:18.

And mount Sinai was altogether on a smoke, because the LORD descended

**upon it in fire: and the smoke thereof
ascended as the smoke of a furnace, and
the whole mount quaked greatly.**

When Pancho read that a mountain trembled at the presence of the living God, he came to the realization that God was real and not a fairy tale. The living God himself had stirred Pancho's heart that night through his word and placed an irresistible burning passion within his heart to find out more about this great God that causes mountains to tremble at his mere presence.

The following day was a Wednesday, and Pancho's parents always went to church on Wednesdays. So, Pancho had decided to go to church with them. While at church, Pancho heard a clear presentation of the gospel of Jesus of Nazareth. When the pastor gave the invitation at the end of the service and said, "If you would like to place your faith and trust in Jesus, please come forward and invite Christ into your heart and ask him to forgive you of all your sins."

Pancho wanted to go but was too embarrassed to go forward in front of strangers. What if someone recognized him? What if someone made fun of him for being in church? He would have to punch them out in church and this just didn't seem right.

Pancho went to church on the following Sunday as well. God was really softening his heart through the praise and worship, personal testimonies, and the sermons. But he was still too embarrassed to go forward and accept Christ as his personal savior.

On the following Wednesday he was getting ready to go to church when his neighbor, close female friend, and drinking buddy, Cross-eyed Mary, who lived directly in front of his parent's house, invited him over to hang out for a few minutes before it was time for him to go. They sat on her front porch enjoying the warm San Antonio evening. Pancho had dressed up a bit and was wearing a thrift store blazer that he had borrowed from his father. Cross-eyed Mary was wearing a revealing tank top and some Daisy Duke blue jean shorts.

The Daisy Duke's must have caught the attention of a young Westsider that was walking down the street with a companion. Pancho could tell these guys were Westsiders because they were wearing khakis pants, tangerine Stacy Adams shoes, white "wife beater" undershirts and a red bandana across their forehead.

The Westsider waved at Cross-eyed Mary and she called him over. The Westsider immediately came over and had begun to flirt with her. Pancho didn't think anything of the matter since this was what Cross-eyed Mary did all the time. The Westsider asked them if they wanted to buy a joint of marijuana. Cross-eyed Mary exuberantly affirmed. Pancho pulled out a dollar bill to pay for the joint, but the Westsider said, "I don't have the marijuana on me. I'll have to go pick it up from around the corner. It will only take me a minute. Don't go anywhere, I'll be right back."

Within three minutes the Westsider returned and gladly handed the joint over to Pancho, took the dollar, and hurriedly vacated the premises. Cross-eyed Mary took the joint from Pancho and hastily lit it up and had begun to take long, deep puffs from it. Each time she inhaled her eyes bulged out. Then she would hold her nose with her left hand and close her eyes in profound satisfaction as she held the smoke within her gasping lungs. She did this several times and Pancho had noticed that the joint was halfway gone so he told her, "Hey, don't Bogart that joint. Pass it around."

She reluctantly handed it to Pancho, snorted twice, and said, "That's some really good stuff."

Pancho thought to himself, "This is great. I'll catch a good buzz, then go and enjoy the church service." He took a puff and had noticed that it tasted peculiar. He took a second puff for further investigation and told Cross-eyed Mary, "This does not taste like weed. I can't put my finger on it exactly, but it definitely is not weed."

He took another puff and had realized that it tasted like tobacco and immediately extinguished the joint and tore it open to physically inspect the mysterious substance.

Pancho was extremely familiar with marijuana and was able to detect the counterfeit. It unquestionably was cigarette tobacco. Cross-eyed Mary kept objecting to Pancho's verdict saying, "It's some good stuff. Look, I've got a buzz already."

Pancho was infuriated that someone would try and pull such a deceptive scam on him. If there was anything that angered Pancho, it was someone taking advantage of him and thinking that he was a chump or a door mat to be stepped upon. This Westsider was obviously not from this neck of the woods and had never heard of Pancho Martinez. Pancho went to church and could not shake the uneasy feeling he had within his stomach from just having someone take advantage of him.

He thought of many ways to retaliate against the Westsider if he ever got his hands on him, but the pastor's sermon was about loving your enemies and forgiving those who have wronged you. Pancho left the church with forgiveness in his heart toward the Westsider and had decided to let it go. After all, it was only a one-dollar swindle.

Two days later, on Friday night at 7:00 P.M., Pancho was hanging out with Cross-eyed Mary on her front porch, his cousin Mando and his girlfriend Ana Belle, and his brother Pistol Pete. They had been drinking a few beers and having some laughs. As they had been talking and enjoying each other's company, the Westsider and his buddy walked in front of the house. Pancho told his cohorts about the incident with the fake joint. They all laughed at Cross-eyed Mary for having fallen for the hoax. Pancho thought about confronting the Westsider but had remembered Jesus' words about love and forgiveness so he let him walk past without any harm.

The Westsider and his buddy must have gone to the local corner store and were making their way back when Pancho noticed a smirk upon the Westsider's face. This caused Pancho to want to act and let the Westsider know that he had caught on to his scam. Pancho told his brother and his cousin, "I'll be back. I'm going to let him know that I know what he did and that he did not fool me. I'm not going to fight with him; I only want him to know that I know."

Pancho walked up to the Westsider and stopped him and said, "Hey man, do you remember me?"

The Westsider replied, "I remember you," and began to laugh.

Pancho thought to himself, "This guy's making fun of me. But I'm not going to fight."

Then Pancho said, "I know what you did. I know that it was cigarette tobacco that you put into the joint."

The Westsider looked at Pancho in the eyes and said, "What are you going to do about it?"

Pancho answered, "I don't want to fight; I only want you to know that I know what you did."

The Westsider said, "You're not going to do anything. You're just a little punk."

Pancho could not believe the brazenness of this guy. The Westsider was either really brave or really stupid. Pancho could no longer restrain himself as he felt his Aztec blood begin to boil and the hair on the back of his neck stand at attention.

The Westsider had crossed the line and mocked Pancho to his face. He looked tough but Pancho was sure he could take him. Pancho faked a straight right to the Westsider's face hoping that he would fall for his con, and he did. The Westsider flinched and raised his left hand to try and block Pancho's rapidly approaching fist but was met with nothing but air. Pancho quickly threw two stiff left hooks to his face and they both connected solidly. He saw the Westsider's eyes roll back in their sockets and then the Westsider went down and hit the hard, black pavement of the dirty city street, "Whack!"

Pancho was not going to stop there; he had to teach this guy a lesson for thinking he was a chump. Pancho kicked the Westsider in the teeth twice, then pounced on top of him and began to do a ground and pound.

Pancho was swinging violently with both fists. The Westsider was screaming, crying, and pleading for Pancho to stop, "Please leave me alone! I beg of you! Please, please! I'll give you your money back, just please stop hitting me!"

Every once in a while, the Westsider would move his

head in order to avoid the blows and Pancho would hit the pavement with his fists. Pancho's hands were full of blood from the guys face and he had not noticed the deep cuts and open gashes on his knuckles from hitting the pavement (he still has the scars to this day). The Westsider's friend had thought about getting involved in the fight for a split second, but Pistol Pete and Mando told him, "Don't even think about it."

The Westsiders friend stayed back out of the way. Pete and Mando had pulled Pancho off of the Westsider and said, "That's enough! He's had enough!"

As they pulled Pancho off of the Westsider, they each threw a kick to the Westsider's already disfigured, bloody face.

On Sunday, Pancho went to church. Each song during the service reminded him of all the horrible, ghastly, and atrocious things he had done in his life. The sermon was about the death of Jesus and it brought Pancho to tears. Pancho had been emotionally stirred, but he had not wanted anyone to see him cry. Pancho had realized at that moment that going to church, believing in God, and life in general was not about being outwardly religious. It was not about putting on a facade or trying to be someone you're not. It was not about being a Baptist, or a Roman Catholic, or a Methodist, or any other type of religious label. Pancho had finally realized that it was all about the person of Jesus!

When the invitation had been given at the end of the service, Pancho could no longer resist. He stood up and verbally stated aloud, "I don't care who sees me or who makes fun of me; I know that I need Jesus and his forgiveness!" Pancho humbly walked down the isle.

THE LAST SIN OF PANCHO MARTINEZ

On that historic Sunday morning, Pancho Martinez, no middle name, plain and simple, had accepted the Lord Jesus Christ as his personal savior. Pancho had become a born again, redeemed by the blood of the lamb, saved from hell and the wrath of God, hallelujah follower of Christ.

After his conversion, Pancho had begun to attend church regularly and was discipled by a faithful and spectacular Sunday school teacher. The Sunday school teacher taught Pancho the basics of Christianity. Pancho was encouraged to memorize scripture and to understand that the Christian life must be practical, Christ-centered, and full of love for God and humanity. Pancho was so immersed in church, bible study, prayer, evangelism, and Christian fellowship that he had not noticed that months had gone by without having taken one drink of alcohol or using any drugs whatsoever. It was a magnificent and new experience for him to live life drug and alcohol free.

2 Corinthians 5:17
Therefore if any man be in Christ, he is a new creature: old things are passed away; behold, all things are become new.

Galatians 2:20
I am crucified with Christ: nevertheless I live; yet not I, but Christ liveth in me: and the life which I now live in the flesh I live by the faith of the Son of God, who loved me, and gave himself for me.

The old Pancho Martinez had died on that Sunday morning when he had accepted Jesus as his personal savior as surmised by these two scriptures. All of Pancho's sins had been forgiven. All of his sins, not just one or two, or just the little white lies, but every single sin was forgiven. Pancho had exchanged his life for the life of Christ.

The new Pancho Martinez was literally given a new chance at life like a newborn baby. His new Christian life involved giving all of his life to Jesus; all his dreams, desires, hopes, plans, and everything that was within him. Being a Christian would make the difference in the way he would approach his career, school, marriage, child-rearing, recreational activities, finances, friends, and on and on and on. It would include every aspect of his life, and every minute of every day.

Pancho used to work for the Pace Picante Company when he was in his late teenage years. His cousins Tudy, and Ronnie worked there as well. All day long they would work with and handle the fresh *jalapeños* and the finished product of hot sauce. They would bottle, inspect, and box the hot sauce through an assembly line. At the end of the day he would totally smell like Pace Picante sauce. He would go home and take a shower and the smell would not go away. He would take two or three showers and nothing.

The hot sauce smell was so deep in his skin, his pores, and his body, that he could not get rid of it. Everywhere he went people would suddenly get hungry and get the urge to eat chips and *salsa*. He would go out on a date, and . . . sniff . . . Pace Picante sauce. He would go to the Movies, and . . . sniff . . . Pace Picante sauce. He would go to the store and . . . sniff . . . Pace Picante sauce. He would go to the bathroom, and . . . sniff . . . Pace Picante sauce.

Christians should be so involved with and immersed in

God that they begin to smell like God. Of course, this is not meant literally but metaphorically. People knew where Pancho worked because of his hot sauce smell. Jesus should be so deep, down in your skin, your pores, your body and your soul, that people should know where you spend your time: with the Master and Lord of all!

Do you smell like God? You should!

Printed in the United States
By Bookmasters